Out of the Ashes

Mitchell Mountain

ISBN: 978-1-7379828-0-7

To Johnny, whose light was dashed away too soon

ACKNOWLEDGMENTS

I would like to thank my good friend, Seth Adelsperger, for his continued support since this was nothing but ramblings on a page. As well as all those who suffered through chunks of this book as I wrote it and shared their thoughts.

PROLOGUE

The Demons' Cavity served as the breeding ground for foul creatures. Fleshlings and bolgias ran rampant across the forsaken wasteland. Tainted, the soil grew infertile, unable to produce a sapling. Dark clouds cast a constant veil over the land, blotting out the sun. Jagged mountain ranges endlessly stretched along the horizon like rows of carnivorous teeth, with the only entrance being a col to the east. A fleshling horde huddled around a small stream, one of three, snaking its way through the ravaged landscape. Three figures, adorned in black cloaks with hoods, sent the demonic creatures scampering upon their approach.

One of the cloaked figures was a goliath with broad shoulders. The other sported lavish curves only visible when the wind hugged the cloak tight to her body. The third hid within his vestment with no discernable features or frame. A ghost masked in darkness. He led the other two deeper into the despairing pit.

A raven descended from the sky and perched itself on the woman's shoulder, rustling its feathers as if to convey a message.

She spoke to the figure guiding them, "Are we sure it's here? My pet has yet to see anything but the typical ghouls."

"We're sure to find it," he said with confidence, striding along the bank with his arms crossed behind his back.

The tall one agreed, "I doubt Indiges would bring us this far to send us on some foolish quest."

The woman turned to her raven. The bird fluffed its wings and cocked its head. "If it is here, it can't be seen from the sky."

The leading figure held up a hand, inspecting it. "That poses no issue."

They continued following the stream, eventually discovering its convergence with the other two at a strange oasis. The small amount of vegetation present withered and browned, losing more color the closer it grew to the water. A singular tree, its branches barren and bark scorched black like charcoal, stood erect at the opposite end. The cold water soaked the bottom of their cloaks as they waded through the pond. The goliath and the woman kept a fair distance as their leader ventured further toward the center. Holding out an arm, particles of black sand swirled within his palm and clumped together, forming an obsidian rock about the size of an apple. He sent it crashing into the water, and the particles burrowed into the ground, disappearing.

A still moment passed as the three figures waited.

The ground trembled, and vibrations echoed through ripples in the water, slowly growing larger. Bubbles foamed a few feet away as a towering structure climbed out from the depths. Water cascaded along its sides decorated in the calligraphy of a language long lost to time. Black sand leaked out from the pillar's base, turning the water into a black lacquer. The strange liquid swarmed around the woman's feet, sending a chill racing up her spine. The sudden sensation withdrew a breath from her lungs. The raven on her shoulder melted into a mist that swirled around her body. The goliath dipped a hand into the liquid, cupping the substance into his palm. It seeped into his skin, turning it pale and his veins black.

The third figure wiped a hand across the stone. A powerful hum coursed through his body, harmonizing with his spirit. He smiled with pride. "I can hear them calling out to me." A numbness expanded throughout his body. It was cold but in a comforting way. He turned back toward the other two. "Send word to the others. The opportunity for acquiring the necessary pieces will soon come. We need to be ready."

1

Blackwood paced the ornate halls of the palace, clad in his formal white tunic and trousers with a navy sash wrapped around his waist. His cape dragged against the marble floors as he nervously stroked his goatee, deep in thought. The possibility of the war coming to an end had him on edge. For the majority of his career, the Red Rebellion never gave an inch, persisting for decades despite the death of two former leaders. Now, they called for a ceasefire and wished to bargain for peace. It was quite the sudden change in tune. It wouldn't be uncharacteristic of them to offer an olive branch in one hand while clutching a hidden blade in the other. Since its inception, the rebellion sought the head of those who would wear the crown. While their forces paled in comparison to the Phoenix Militia, they proved elusive and cunning, utilizing guerilla tactics to shed blood across the continent for decades. Some argued they were reaching a precipice to turn the tide of the war entirely in their favor. If that was true, then why negotiate for peace?

The more his mind pondered these troubling thoughts, the more uneasy he felt. Fear twisted the possibility of this meeting being nothing more than a ruse to usurp the king and topple Parliament into a reality.

A voice echoed down the hallway, "Blackwood."

The intruding thoughts went silent as Blackwood's gaze snapped up from the floor. Glowing in the light from the stained-glass windows was Peter Clougher, King of Argust. At the twilight of his life, he held the stature and confidence of a young warrior. He approached wearing a navy-blue tail coat with black trim, wrapped in a cloak clasped around his collar by a phoenix-shaped pendant. The metal brace clinging to his right knee rattled as he hurried past Blackwood.

"Everyone is awaiting your presence," Blackwood informed.

"Of all the days for this damned brace to give me trouble," cursed the king. "I might as well replace my entire leg like Lawson."

"With respect," said Blackwood, "I still have suspicions about these negotiations." The wrinkles on Peter's brow furrowed deeper, but the king always appreciated his chancellor's counsel. "While I am elated for this war to come to an end, I'm still not entirely convinced this act is genuine. What reason do they have for wanting peace? More followers rally to their cause each day, we've yet to discover their base of operations, and their rallying cry has always been to take the heads of you and your children."

"A bit late for debates," Peter retorted.

"Just be cautious. This feels like a trick."

The king stopped walking, causing Blackwood to stumble. Peter turned, and his ocean-blue eyes consumed the chancellor in a wave of pain. It was the look of a weary man, chipped away by conflict and age. Desperation stared at Blackwood through the king's glistening eyes like a stranger through a window.

"I understand your concern," Peter said softly, "but this war has taken its toll on the land and its people for far too long. I'll be damned if this conflict continues to plague my family. If this is a chance for it to end, it must be seized." He placed a firm hand on Blackwood's shoulder. "I need you to stand by my side."

Peter spoke to him not as the king but as a friend. They faced many tribulations throughout their years working together, cleaning up the mistakes of their predecessors in an attempt to better the kingdom. In some ways, they had, and in others, they failed, but Peter's determination remained undeterred. After the birth of his first daughter, the king wished to hand over a kingdom at peace and brimming with prosperity, unlike the one he was born into.

"Always." Blackwood's voice did not falter.

Smiling, Peter proceeded down the hall. In that moment, all of Blackwood's doubts vanished. Like the ancient Order of the Saints, he would follow his king into battle no matter the cost.

Rushing after him, they approached a set of large, oak doors. A pair of Militia soldiers stood guard, their blue uniforms adorned with a white phoenix on their backs. They saluted as the two men passed.

The doors opened to reveal the Great Hall, a spacious room with high, arched ceilings and a sea of tables. While these seats were usually filled with chattering aristocrats and politicians, this time, they remained vacant. Gathered at the head of the room was a small group whose eyes were trained on them.

Seated on the far-right was the rebellion's leader, Reed Skokna. Her sleek, ebony hair and slender face provided a vibrant beauty hiding her true, monstrous nature. Lingering over her shoulder was a bald-headed man with a worn, leather husk of a face. Elliot Durham, a former ambassador, turned traitor, earned himself a new title as high overseer and second in command after changing allegiances. At their flanks were two other men dressed in ratty, brown clothing. Red bands wrapped around their arms, giving the rebellion its namesake. They claimed it as a symbol for their fallen brethren, who died under the rule of Peter's father, King Lucius II. Their presence within the palace walls made Blackwood's skin crawl.

Relief swept over him as his eyes shifted to the other end of the table, landing on the familiar face of Kaylin Gunnway. Her long, golden hair was pulled back into a ponytail, revealing her bony cheeks and pointed chin. Unlike the soldiers next to her, she dawned a blue high-collar padded jacket lined with leather buckles signifying her rank as a division captain. She was not only skilled with a blade but also one of the few augmented by the traditions of old. Her presence guaranteed the king's safety during this exchange. Climbing the stairs, Blackwood greeted her with a slight nod.

"We were beginning to think you'd gotten lost," Reed chimed across the table. "Must be difficult to find your way without a map."

The king no longer radiated with the intensity from before, wearing the veil of a dotting old man. "Forgive me," he said. "Getting around seems to become more difficult each day." He motioned to the brace hugging his knee as he collapsed into his chair. The gap between them was almost as great as the difference in age. Reed was at the tail end of her prime, while the king's years were visible in the silvers of his hair.

The rebel leader leaned back in her chair, tossing her raven locks over her shoulder. "Well, we're glad you finally made it and for graciously allowing us into the capital. It's the first time we're witnessing its grandeur."

Peter chuckled. "It is beautiful." His wrinkles folded over themselves as he grinned. "I often find myself taking it for granted from time to time. It was quite unexpected to hear you call for a ceasefire."

"This war has gone on for long enough, shedding plenty of blood on our side," said Reed, "and yours as well, I'm sure."

The king crossed his arms, wearing a solemn expression.

"Unfortunately, that is true. More unfortunate that it took until now for you to come to the table."

Reed's ruby red lips curled into a devilish smile. "It did take some time. Time I spent thinking and realizing that this war was one passed down to us by our fathers. Neither of us wanted it. Just because they hated each other doesn't mean we have to."

Peter raised a brow. "I hope you will prove your words true through action."

Elliot Durham stepped forward. "We are prepared to resign our forces to the western estuaries where we wish to rule as a sovereign state, independent of the kingdom and its laws, with our own governing body." His voice was rough as steel-grinding stone.

Blackwood clenched his jaw as each word drilled into his ears. After the traitor finished his statement, the chancellor lowered himself to offer counsel to the king. "If they wish for land, we can give them Takata. No one has settled there for years."

With a flick of his finger, Peter dismissed Blackwood. His gaze returned to the rebels and said, "That is a reasonable request. If you wish to settle along the estuaries, we can offer you the land where Takata once flourished."

"With all due respect, Your Majesty," said Reed. "We were looking more southward, establishing along the coastline near Bushgrove."

This concerned Blackwood. The open fields north of the

estuaries were vast, granting the rebels plenty of land as well as leaving a healthy border between them and any nearby cities of the kingdom. Bordering a large town like Bushgrove seemed too close for comfort. Soon enough, they would wish to expand, and that expansion could lead to another outbreak of conflict.

Blackwood bent down to whisper his thoughts to Peter.

"Done," the king said before Blackwood could utter a word. "You will gain sovereignty over the lands south of Bushgrove along the coastline. Four million acres should be satisfactory."

"Your Majesty," muttered Blackwood. "It would be wise to first consult—"

Peter silenced him with a raised finger. "Do you have any qualms about my offer?"

"You are most fair," said Elliot with an awkward bow.

Reed remained still in her chair, staring at them with her piercing green eyes. She tapped her chin with a slender finger as if lost in thought. "You do present a pleasant offer. Agreed. We shall pull back our forces to the western coast immediately."

Blackwood could scarcely believe the war lasting decades had come to such a swift and calm end.

"We should share a toast," roared the rebel leader. "To celebrate the prosperity for us both."

The king beckoned for chalices of wine to be fetched. Thorns wrapped around Blackwood's stomach with such intensity he needed to lean against the table for support, but no one seemed to notice. Glancing over his shoulder, Blackwood saw that

Kaylin appeared calm and stoic, but the intense look in her eyes told him everything. This pain was not the result of some strange illness, but his gut screaming to him that something was wrong.

Cries of panic erupted outside the hall's doors. A soldier barged in, red-faced and covered in sweat. His arrival sent both sides reaching for their weapons.

"Your Majesty," the soldier yelled, "intruders have set fire to the north side of the palace. Sellswords or assassins of some kind."

Peter took command of the room. "I apologize for the inconvenience, Miss Skokna, but it would be best if we sought safety."

Reed calmly rose from her seat. "My men can escort me out of the palace. Such a shame. I was really hoping to share some good wine." She strutted down the stairs, followed by Elliot and their rebel troops. Peter, focused on the dilemma at hand, dismissed their casual behavior, but Blackwood watched them leave with a critical glare as the knot in his stomach tightened.

Kaylin stepped between Peter and Blackwood. "It'd be best to seek shelter in the Tomb. Until the fire and intruders are dealt with."

They agreed and chased her down the stairs with two Militia soldiers covering their flank. Beyond the oak doors, people fled to the southern end of the palace as soldiers directed them to safety, some even running in the opposite direction. They raced through the halls into a vacant corridor and toward the iron-clad door of the Chamber of Parliament, more often referred to as the Tomb. An ancient section of the palace built from stone, it served as the meeting place for ambassadors to discuss issues concerning the realm. Kaylin forced the door open, and they descended a spiraling staircase into the menacing, stone chamber. At the center, nine thrones encircled a chasm glowing with fire that cast the edges of the room into darkness.

Blackwood placed himself in one of the thrones; the stone rubbed smooth from the many previous Parliament members who sat in them before. Peter ambled toward one of the other thrones, resting. The dash from the Great Hall left him winded. "My daughters are safe?" he wheezed to Kaylin.

"In the upper chambers with at least ten guards," the Militia captain assured.

Relieved, the king sank deeper into his seat.

Suddenly, the two Militia soldiers dropped to the ground, lifeless. Blood seeped out from their necks and into the cracks of the floor, weaving its way toward Blackwood and the king. Kaylin unsheathed the two sabers clinging to her hips.

"Step out of the shadows," she demanded, pointing one of the blades into the black void. A pair of milky, white eyes penetrated through the darkness. A shiver crawled down Blackwood's spine as an assassin, shrouded in a gray hood, emerged. Various blades and mechanisms lining his waist and gauntlets clanged with each step he took.

"Captain Gunnway." His voice lingered in the air like a

chilling fog. He brandished a jagged, silver sword. "This may be less dreary than I originally anticipated."

"Who are you?" the Militia captain demanded. Her knuckles turned white, clutching the hilt of the sabers.

The stranger remained silent with only a crooked smirk peeking out from beneath his hood. He took a swift step forward, swinging his blade at Kaylin, who caught it with her own. The two proceeded to clash in a song of steel as sparks ignited around them. Blackwood could barely follow the pace of the two combatants moving like specters, phasing through the other's attacks. The chamber seemed to quake with each exchanged blow. Kaylin retorted with a flurry of strikes, all of which the assassin either evaded or batted away. Light on his feet, the man disengaged with a back step and hurled a metal pellet at the ground. Shattering in an explosion of light, it blinded Kaylin as the assassin plunged his blade deep into her side. Her sabers clattered to the floor as she collapsed.

The hooded man towered over the defenseless captain. Her bloodied hands covered the wound as she struggled to stand. Blackwood launched out of the stone seat, leaping for one of the dead soldiers' swords, but a well-placed dagger pierced his thigh, causing him to tumble.

"Your turn will come soon enough, Chancellor," hissed the assassin. "There is still your beloved captain to deal with." He straddled Kaylin, gripping a strong hand around her neck and holding her down. Blackwood pulled the dagger from his leg,

13

his white trousers stained red with blood. Looking up, he could see a row of decaying teeth smile at her as the assassin dangled the point of his jagged blade just over her head. As it crashed down, another hand grabbed the assassin's wrist. Peter placed one of Kaylin's blades against his throat. Even at his advanced age, he could still move swiftly when needed.

"Release her," Peter commanded, "or your blood will be the next to stain these floors."

The assassin relaxed his grip on the sword as the king took it, forcing him to stand. Kaylin staggered to her feet, blood dripping from her side. She retrieved the other saber and pointed it at the assassin's chest, prepared to thrust. Blackwood fumbled for the dead soldier's blade. A bolt of pain shot up from his leg as he hobbled to join Kaylin and Peter.

"I'll ask again," said Kaylin, "who are you?"

The assassin responded with a chilling cackle. With his head raised, the shroud of his hood lifted, revealing the muted color of his decomposed flesh around the eyes, nose, and mouth. He resembled a corpse more than a man.

"Well, well," the hooded man said. "Seems you're not as weak as you let on, old man. Looks like I underestimated you." With a twitch of his hand, two more pellets exploded in flashes of light. As Kaylin, Peter, and Blackwood's eyes strained to regain sight, they discovered that the assassin escaped.

Peter wrapped an arm around Kaylin as he ripped off his cloak to cover the wound. "Blackwood, are you alright?"

Blackwood finished tying a bit of cloth from his cape around his leg wound. "I'm fine."

"Then help me with Captain Gunnway," Peter commanded.

Blackwood provided support on her other side, and the two men proceeded to climb the spiral staircase with Kaylin slung over their shoulders. It was challenging as the wound ached with each step, but Blackwood ignored it. He had no right to complain as the captain bled out in their arms.

"Thank you," Kaylin said. "If you hadn't intervened, I'd be dead."

"You've been protecting me for more than ten years now," the king said with a warm smile. "It's about time I returned the favor."

"Who was that assassin?" Blackwood interjected. "His strength, agility, reflexes, not to mention skill with a blade, were a match even for you."

"He's obviously been augmented by implants," Kaylin said, wincing in pain. "His face was a clear sign of REV overdose."

The haunting image of the assassin's decaying face crept back into Blackwood's mind. What frightened him most was it seemed recognizable. He searched his memories, flipping through the many faces he had encountered throughout his life, like pages in a book. A man with skin barely clinging to his face should be hard to forget, yet nothing breached his memory. Then, Blackwood remembered his eyes. Those piercing, white eyes stained his memory. He'd seen them only once before. The revelation paralyzed him with fear. Kaylin grunted in agony as Peter kept walking, stretching the wound.

"We've got to keep moving," the king barked.

"I've seen that man before," Blackwood whispered. Peter and Kaylin stared at him in shock. "During my years as Chancellor Valcrum's steward, I remember seeing a man in passing with those eyes. His face wasn't so decrepit, but that menacing gaze. Even for the brief moment they glanced my way, they chilled me to the bone. Chancellor Valcrum wrote in his personal records that he was hired to kill the rebellion's original leader, Richard Skokna."

Peter urged him to continue climbing the staircase, posing the question, "Who possesses the means of hiring such a man? A sellsword of that caliber doesn't come cheap, and how is it he infiltrated the Tomb knowing we would be here?"

Blackwood had his suspicions, given how casually the rebels seemed to leave the Great Hall, but it was foolish to toss out accusations without evidence. The matter required further investigation.

"Whoever it was most likely coordinated the attack with the other intruders," Kaylin added. "No doubt they were used as a means to force us into the Tomb to be ambushed." If that was true, then whoever staged the attempt on the king's life procured knowledge shared with only high-status nobles, Militia personnel, and the ambassadors."

Unlatching the iron door, they exited the Tomb and entered

the vacant corridor. A handful of soldiers rounded a nearby corner and, in seeing Kaylin injured, raced to her aid.

"Your Majesty," one of them said.

"Take Captain Gunnway to the infirmary," Peter commanded. Two of them unloaded Kaylin from the king and Blackwood's shoulders and carried her down the hall. With his protector cared for, Peter turned to another soldier. "What of the intruders?"

"They've been killed, Your Majesty, and the fire has been put out. Your daughters are safe, and the rebels were unharmed in their escape."

The king nodded before staring back at the soldier with icy blue eyes. "A hooded assassin attacked us in the Tomb and nearly killed Captain Gunnway. He was able to escape, so I want you to rally more men and search the palace for him."

"Sire." The soldier bowed and sprinted off to bid his king's command.

Peter turned to Blackwood with a grave expression. "You probably need to visit the infirmary as well."

"Later," said Blackwood. "Right now, word needs to be sent out to the other ambassadors. We'll make this assassin the most wanted man across the continent."

"You remember the man's name?" asked Peter.

He did. Blackwood could see it etched in his predecessor's handwriting before his very eyes. He spat out the name as if it were deadly poison. "Vargo. Vargo Vasallo."

2

The shadows of the metal bars across the windows in the Muddy Mule reminded Anden more of a prison cell than a tavern. A bit fitting, given that the usual patrons consisted of bandits, sellswords, and other scum seeking refuge from the Militia within the capital's walls. He slumped over the bar, nursing the last bit of his whiskey in his flask. Cuts, burns, and bullet holes branded its surface. He knew the story behind each one. If it wasn't a mark he personally witnessed, he'd heard the tale a thousand times over from the tavern's owner, Eli, at least before the raggedy, old bastard held a grudge against him.

"Looking to fill up, Andy?" a voice sang.

Anden lifted his head to see the amber curls of Stacey, a middle-aged barmaid who clung to the remnants of her youth. She was pretty for her age, and the aid of a corset pushing her breasts to her chin certainly helped.

"You think that to be a good idea?" asked Anden. "You'd be

going against your boss's wishes. I'm lucky he still lets me into this place."

"If that cranky geezer catches you, then tell him I paid for it." Stacey's fondness for him seemed boundless. For Anden to say he didn't take advantage of it on occasion would be a lie. At times, he wondered if that fondness stretched far enough to enter her bed, but such curiosity fell short of any action. Finishing the last few drops, he slid the empty flask over to her.

"Homebrew is all I can do for you," she said.

Anden's mouth twisted into a frown. Eli's homebrew liquor tasted foul, lingering on one's tongue until the next morning. He longed for the dash of honey contained within the nectar of a fine Bushgrove whiskey, but liquor of that quality seemed rarer than gold these days. For no apparent reason, the manufacturers of high-quality liquor raised their prices to rake in more coin from extravagant, wealthy nobles and the establishments they frequented, and it worked. Unable to afford keeping such drinks in stock, humble establishments similar to the Muddy Mule needed to produce their own brews of liquor and ale to stay in business. Unfortunately for their patrons, it paled in comparison to the once-affordable Bushgrove, Laminfell, and Sandur brands.

Stacey returned from behind the bar and handed Anden the refilled flask. A bony hand caught her wrist. Eli stood next to her; his bugling right eye twitched in anger. His wrinkled, old skin cracked as he grimaced at them. The tavern's owner was a stubborn fossil of a man who, throughout the years, earned the respect of many cutthroats acting as members of the three gangs ruling over the capital's southeast district. It was that respect the elder needed to maintain, therefore turning his once warm heart into cold stone after Anden compiled a tab he couldn't pay back.

"Whatcha think yer doing?" he said. "This one has a debt needing to get paid, and 'til then, he won't get a drop."

Anden fished out a few copper coins from his pocket, slamming them onto the bar. "This is all I have to offer at the current moment."

Seeing the copper pieces, Eli kept his hand locked around Stacey's wrist. "Those won't cut it. Unless they're rusted gold pieces."

"I'm covering the cost of this one," barked Stacey, ripping her arm free. "He can't buy his own drinks, but you didn't say anything about others buying them for him."

The old man begrudgingly scooped the coins into his hand. He held his ground against any mercenary or thief, but Stacey had something about her, as most women do. Any stranger would think she ran the bar, and they would be right for the most part. Eli left Anden to his drink, muttering obscenities under his breath.

Anden unscrewed the cap of the flask and forced the homebrew liquor down his gullet. There was no initial flavor, only the burning sensation that singed his nostrils and watered his eyes, followed by an aftertaste that contorted his face into a sour expression. It was the type of drink serving one purpose—to get piss drunk. Unfortunately, it took more than most for him to achieve such a level of intoxication.

"Thanks, Stacey," he said, pulling his lips free from the flask. "If it weren't for you, Eli would probably have every man in here gutting me right on the bar."

"Just work on paying him back," she said. "Even though it may not seem like it, he still likes you. It's just he can't have customers skimping out on their tabs in this part of town."

Anden tipped his hat to her. "In that case, I guess I owe both of you now."

"Then, you better pay me back quickly. Emperor help you if I start to get angry like Eli." She gave him a soft smile and a wink before strutting down the bar.

Anden returned to his drink, wincing with every sip. At a nearby table, a group of rugged men wearing dark leather jackets with bone-hilted swords strapped to their hips murmured amongst themselves. Turning an ear in their direction, Anden overheard their conversation.

"You seen the reward on the newest member of the Militia's hit list?" said one of the men. "It's worth more gold than the Burnt Coat or the Hand of Death."

"Don't be getting any ideas." The one speaking loomed above the others as he leaned closer over the table. "Rumor among the higher-ups is that he nearly killed the king and wounded Gunnway in the process. I heard he's the best sword money can buy."

"Come on, Cronin. You don't actually think I'd be stupid enough to hunt a bounty like that. It's just interesting to see the Hand of Death finally get knocked off his top spot. Never thought I'd see it, honestly." The man gulped down his tankard of ale. "Though, I suppose he has been quiet over the past few years."

"Any word on who might've hired the assassin?" asked one of the other men sitting at the table.

The big one, Cronin, responded, "None that's worth a damn. As far as the crown's concerned, we could've hired him."

"Do in a day what the rebellion couldn't in years. Sounds like the higher-ups' style." They all erupted in laughter, enjoying their drinks.

The front door creaked open, catching everyone's attention. The thugs around the table, along with Anden, turned to see the new patron. A woman wrapped in a maroon cloak embroidered with gold trimmings stepped into the tavern. The hood glanced about the room at their gawking faces before shuffling to a nearby table. Stacey hurried over and took the woman's order. She prepared a cup of tea with a thin wisp of steam trailing behind her as she delivered it to the mysterious stranger. Strange for someone with wealth to enter a watering hole for lowlifes, but it wasn't any of Anden's business.

A large fist crashed into the bar, shaking it. It was the leader of the thugs from before. His giant-like body was shaped like a keg, and the only discernible features poking through his thicket of facial hair were a wide, stunted nose and a pair of bronze-colored eyes. A vile odor emitted from his body, crawling into Anden's nostrils, making them flare in disgust.

"Need another round at our table soon," he said, wiping his scraggly beard dry. "We're starting to run low."

"When are you going to produce some coin?" asked Eli. "You've had a few rounds already, and not a single piece has made its way into my hand."

Light flickered off the steel of the large man's dagger as he unsheathed it. He twirled it in his hand, making sure Eli could see the bone-crafted handle. "You know who I work for, so the coin will come. I guarantee it." He stabbed the blade into the bar's surface, glaring at Anden. "Unlike this one here who needs the bar wench to pay for his drinks."

"Careful calling the lady a wench," said Anden. He disregarded the insult with a drink from his flask. "Unless you want a tankard shoved up your ass."

Cronin lumbered over, his massive size eclipsing the light over Anden entirely. His thick brow furrowed in a mixture of amusement and annoyance. "Seems the scrawny man has quite the pair to be threatening me."

The rest of his men sat on the edge of their seats, grins twisting their faces.

"Threat. No, no. A mere warning. I've seen Stacey kick many a sellsword's ass for calling her a wench." Anden lifted the flask for another drink, but the giant snatched it from his grasp.

"Is this what you were planning to shove up my ass?" taunted Cronin.

Anden extended a hand. "If you would be so kind as to give that back. As shit as the liquor is, I'd hate to waste it."

Cronin's massive hand snatched his tunic and hurled him to the floor. The giant tipped the flask over, dousing Anden in the homebrew. It soaked into his hat along with the rest of his clothes. Thunderous guffaws filled the tavern from Cronin's men as Anden lay there, motionless. Fighting would stir up unwanted attention. Avoiding the Phoenix Militia was enough on its own. He didn't want to worry about the Bone Blades as well. With the last bit dripping from the flask's neck, Cronin tossed it on the ground and returned to his table. His men displayed their approval with pats on his arm as he walked past them.

Stacey hopped over the bar, racing to Anden's side. "You all right, Andy?"

"Yeah." Anden stood up, dripping wet. He picked up his flask, placing it in his pocket and shook his bucket-shaped hat free of any stubborn droplets.

"Hey, wench," Cronin called. "We need that next round."

Stacey was visibly heated, but Anden placed a hand on her shoulder to calm her down. "Be sure to spit in their drinks for me," he whispered before padding out of the tavern, shoulders hunched over. As he headed out, the hooded woman caught his eye. Although her face was hidden, he recognized a judgmental stare.

Outside the tavern, the slums of Alastair's southeast district greeted him. Decrepit buildings piled onto each other in a maze of mud-ridden streets filled with the degenerates of society. When the nobility wiped the shit off their boots, this is where it ended up. Many thieves, mercenaries, and criminals called this region of the capital home. It was the only place within the great wall that offered sanctuary for such scum from the Militia as the soldiers were corrupt and paid off by the three guilds of the underground.

Anden rested on a nearby bench. The heat of the sun shining bright overhead baked the rancid smell of Eli's homebrew into his clothes. Folding his arms, he tipped his head forward so his hat obscured his face as if he were sleeping. He heard the door to the Muddy Mule open, followed by the scent of ocean water crashing against the shore. He recognized it to be perfume, deducing the person wearing it to be the hooded woman.

"Ditch the cloak," he said without raising his head to look at her. "No one around here wears anything embroidered. Not unless they want it to get stolen, or worse."

"Is that so?" Her words were sharp, but her tone was soft. The weight of the bench shifted as she sat next to him. "Please, educate me more."

"Don't get cheeky," he scoffed.

"I'm serious," she said. "I've never ventured to this part of the city before."

He peeked from under the brim of his hat at her. "You could've skipped out on the perfume, and hopefully, you're not wearing any fine jewelry underneath that hood."

She studied her empty hands. "Seems I forgot those back home."

"Then, I would suggest going back for them and never returning to this district," Anden advised.

"How considerate, but I have no intention of returning home at the current moment. Instead, I was looking for a way to leave the capital. Any advice on doing that?"

Anden raised his head to get a clearer look at her. The cloak poured over her shoulders, covering her body. The only visible feature was a pair of pink lips resting on a rounded chin. She was most likely younger than him. By how much was still to be determined.

"Buy a horse," he said. "If you can't afford that, your next best shot is to bribe a traveling merchant of some kind to take you along his next stop. Though, I doubt you'll find one around here that'll make for a trustworthy travel companion. As I said, your best bet is just going back home to your fancy estate. I don't know what you're running from, but it can't be as bad as this shithole."

She gazed out in the direction of the wall looming over the rest of the city. "I'm not really running from anything. I just want to see the continent. I've read so much but seen none of it."

"I'm sure those books painted a scenic landscape of the continent. Let me save you the time. It's not all that it's cracked up to be. Most of what's beyond that wall is more of what you see before you now, and in some places, even worse."

"I don't believe that." She added a chill to her voice. "I believe there's a beautiful world out there, and I'm going to see it all."

Anden rolled his eyes and lowered his head again. "Good luck on your travels, then."

The tavern door burst open once more. This time it was Cronin and his band of thugs. The giant paused for a moment, catching a glimpse of Anden and the hooded woman sitting on the bench. "Found yourself another wench, huh? And this one seems fancy." His eyes undressed her, tracing over the visible outline of her body in the fabric. "Those are some nice threads."

A meaty hand reached for her, but she slapped it away.

"If you showed some respect, you might have better luck with women," said Anden. Cronin swung his arm, planting a fist on Anden, which sent him crashing to the ground. Two of Cronin's lackeys grabbed the woman and tried to tear the cloak off. She flailed and fought but failed to escape their grapple.

"Make sure to search for any coin, too," Cronin ordered. "She's bound to have some on her." He turned his hairy face back to Anden, who climbed to his feet. "You're tough for a scrawny lad. The next time you go down, you'll stay there."

Brandishing the bone-crafted dagger, he thrust it at Anden's chest. In one fluid motion, Anden dodged the blade with a spin and delivered a swift kick to the giant's bloated gut. In a painful gasp for air, he collapsed to one knee. Anden struck Cronin across the temple with the point of his elbow, knocking him out cold.

"Boss," one of the men shouted.

Two of them withdrew their swords and darted toward Anden. They swung recklessly, unable to land a single blow as he weaved between their strikes. With a punch to the throat, one of them collapsed in a fit of coughing, while the other received a solid knee to the groin. The ones restraining the woman released her and charged as well. Anden dealt with them just as quickly, offering them the same fate as their comrades. Standing over the mess of groaning bodies, he surveyed the situation, hands on his hips and with a troubled face.

"Shit," he uttered under his breath. The woman remained where the thugs left her, awestruck. "What coin do you have?" he asked her.

She stammered for words, "Uh, a few gold pieces and a fair bit of silver and copper."

"You said you were looking for transportation. You just found some." Having bested members of the Bone Blades, Anden marked himself among the criminal elites. The southeast district would no longer act as a sanctuary. His only option was to escape beyond the wall, and now he could make a profit doing it.

"Fifteen silver, and I'll take you as far as Lundur right now."

The woman hesitated before answering, "Fine."

"Then come on," Anden demanded, marching down the streets.

As the day waned and they neared the city's edge, everything grew dark. Alastair's wall, stretching one hundred fifty feet into the sky, cast a long shadow, almost turning day into night. Once considered a sign of cowardice under the reign of Harrod II, it now symbolized power as an impenetrable defense. Anden maneuvered through the darkness with the woman straggling behind him like a shadow.

"Hurry up," he spat over his shoulder. She quickened her pace until her feet rubbed against his heels.

"Hey," she said, "if you could fight like that, why didn't you do so in the bar earlier? Instead, you let those guys humiliate you."

Anden gazed at her in an apathetic manner as they traveled through a narrow alley. "You really are a naïve noble girl. The true law of the southeast district are the three guilds. Crossing any of them will put a bounty on your head amid a sea of mercenaries. That lot I left lying in the dirt were members of the Bone Blades, and their leader is not a forgiving one. Just be happy you now have a way out of the capital."

They approached a rust-infested shack about the size of a horse stable. An entanglement of chains wrapped around the front, held together by a lock. Anden removed a ring with three keys from his trouser pocket and unlocked the chains, stripping them from the stable. Sliding the metal sheet door aside, he found his trusty steed. A mangled body of metal with four wheels and a row of seats in the front and back rested before them.

The woman lit up, seeing the pile of scraps. "This is one of those mechanical chariots—the ones that move without a horse. It's in a bit of a rougher shape than the few others I've seen. Are you an engineer of some kind?"

"Not a chance." Anden hopped into one of the front seats with a smaller wheel in place before him and a series of pedals at his feet. "I won it in a bet. Now get in. You're not paying me to answer questions."

Jamming another key into a slot and twisting it, the heap of metal roared to life. Puffs of black smoke sputtered out from the back. The woman crawled into the seat next to him as he adjusted two levers on the small wheel. Pushing another pedal, the chariot surged forward as he steered it. Speeding through the streets, a gust of wind ripped the embroidered hood off the woman's head. A stream of chocolate hair spilled over her shoulders as she glanced over with shocked, hazel eyes. Her complexion was like brush strokes against a canvas, forming a work of art. Anden was speechless, caught in a daze. Pulling the hood back over her head, Anden snapped out of the trance in time to notice their approach upon one of the many gates. He obscured his face with his hat, and the woman clutched the hood tighter over her head. The guards let them pass, not making any move to stop them. Passing through the gate, Anden slammed his foot onto one of the pedals, sending the chariot racing off toward the horizon.

3

Blackwood's head hung over his shoulders like a boulder precariously on the edge of a cliff. Bags weighted down his eyelids. His hair and beard grew mangled and greasy. A good night's sleep evaded him as the assassin's sinister shroud haunted his dreams. It was the same every time. He would struggle, helplessly bound to one of the Tomb's thrones, as Vargo sauntered forward, wielding his jagged blade. Blood seeped from the cracks of the stone floor, turning into a vast, red ocean. Before the fatal blow could be dealt, Blackwood awoke, gripped by the same fear he felt that day.

"Emperor be praised. You look like shit, Blackwood." The heavyset man sitting across the chancellor's desk studied him with a critical eye. Rahm Krawczyk was the ambassador to the kingdom's second division and possessed a cunning mind. While their opinions differed on many subjects, they both believed in the protection and prosperity of the kingdom.

"These past few nights have proved tireless," said Blackwood. "Brookshire has been up my ass about the land promised to the rebels by the king without her counsel, and I've also been dealing with an investigation on who hired Vargo."

"Which has been fruitless, I assume." Rahm's spectacles gleamed in the light as he spoke. He had a knack for reading people. It's what made him a formidable adversary. "Forgive me, but I don't expect you summoned me simply for a friendly chat. You need my help."

"Yes," breathed Blackwood. He ran a hand through his peppered hair. "I am in need of your assistance. Perhaps you can find something I have missed."

The ambassador leaned forward in his chair, pensive. "Have there been whispers from the underground?"

"Speculations and superstitions. Apparently, it was widely believed that Vargo had been dead."

"And the other sellswords?" asked Rahm.

"Nameless," said Blackwood. "Common thugs who could've been hired by anyone. They were only a distraction."

Rahm rubbed a pudgy hand against the bulb of his chin. "If they initiated the fire on the north end of the palace and Vargo awaited you in the Tomb, then it might be fair to presume they each entered a different way."

"How?" groaned the chancellor. "We have guards stationed at every conceivable entrance and at various points throughout the palace. Some stations were even doubled knowing the rebels would be here."

Rahm rose from his seat and sauntered toward the corner of the room where a small bookshelf resided. Running a finger along the spines, he removed one with a worn, tawny cover and rifled through the stained, sheepskin pages. It took a minute as the tome was well-fed with the kingdom's history. He presented Blackwood with a diagram of the palace long before the wall was built, mapping the underground mines once used to collect gold ore.

"Sleeplessness has slowed my mind," said Blackwood. "What are you alluding to?" His patience wore thin for cryptic conversation.

Rahm traced a finger along the web of passages. "One of the tunnels connects to the lower levels of the palace, right below the Tomb."

Blackwood studied the page. "Even so, the ancient gold mines have been caved in for centuries. The landscape has changed so much you'd have difficulty finding one of the entrances, and that's with the help of this map. You expect me to believe a hired sword managed to stumble across one and clear a path as well?"

"Indulge me for a moment," Rahm said with a smirk. "When you left the Tomb that day carrying Gunnway on your shoulder, was the door latched?"

Blackwood entered the sanctum of his mind and roamed the halls of his memories until he remembered climbing the spiral staircase. He could see the door come into view as he ascended with Kaylin in tow. His arm reached out and fumbled to unlock the latch, which could only be locked from the inside.

"Yes," he muttered. "If I remember correctly, the door was latched."

Rahm placed a heavy hand on Blackwood's desk as he leaned in close. "Which leads me to conclude that Vargo used the tunnels to sneak in and out."

The chancellor combed his beard in thought. "It's certainly worth investigating."

"I agree," said Rahm. The desk groaned as he pushed off it. "We should look into it together with Captain Green. If the pathway has been cleared, who knows what we'll find down there."

Blackwood shivered at the thought of Vargo still lurking in the underground tunnels beneath them. With Kaylin still recovering from her injuries, Green was the next best candidate to face such a monster. "Fair enough," he agreed. "It will have to wait until later in the day. I still have other responsibilities to attend."

"Of course." Rahm gave a slight bow. "Get some rest too. At this rate, you'll age faster than the king." He escorted himself out of Blackwood's office.

Climbing out of his chair, Blackwood ambled toward the singular window overlooking the city. The white buildings of various shapes and sizes stretched for miles reaching the base of the wall. Even from his perch, the landscape beyond remained hidden behind the colossal structure. Only the radiance of the capital filled his vision. Carriages rolled through the intricate roadways, each heading to its own destination. Children sprinted through the masses, causing mischief. Militia soldiers searched for ways to pass the time as they stood guard around the palace. It was easy for Blackwood to get lost in his work that he often forgot what the kingdom he helped rule was like.

His door creaked open, and Blackwood spun around to see Mary Katherine Brown standing at the threshold. Despite her advancing age, the first division ambassador's beauty did not spoil. Her eyes were a dull blue, not as radiant as the king's, but the small wrinkles around them enhanced their sparkle. While the sun's light died reaching the day's end, hers did not.

"How did the meeting with Rahm go?" she asked.

"Better than I anticipated." He trudged back to his desk, collapsing into the chair.

Mary Katherine's short cape billowed as she briskly crossed the room. She shifted the chair Rahm sat in closer to his side. "You need to sleep," she said with a sympathetic stare.

"It's not like I haven't tried," he replied. He didn't mean to sound brash, but weariness stifled his mind, allowing the words to fly out heedlessly.

She picked up a leather-bound book resting on his desk, recognizing it as Chancellor Valcrum's personal journal. "Valcrum didn't write any additional information on Vargo?"

"Only mention of him is his commission to assassinate Skokna. After that, he was never seen again."

"And now he's gone from killing the leader of a rebellion to a king." She snapped the book closed, placing it back on his desk. "Or tried."

The map of the mines still lay bare in front of Blackwood on his desk. "May I ask for your counsel on something?"

Mary Katherine nodded.

"How do you suspect Vargo infiltrated the palace?"

Pondering the question, she pulled her oak-brown hair over her shoulder. "Personally, I think someone helped sneak them all in. A spy inside the palace granting them access."

"That's not out of the question," said Blackwood. "Not yet anyway. Rahm proposed Vargo snuck in through one of the mining tunnels."

She raised a brow at that. "But they're—"

"Caved in," he interjected. "I thought so too. Rahm has managed to convince me otherwise, and we're going to look into it later in the night." He sighed a defeated breath. His strength diminished with every passing moment. Fatigue sent him drifting to the brink of slumber, where dreams and reality intermingle, making one unaware of time and unsure whether their recent actions actually happened or not. He shook the feeling off, waking himself.

Mary Katherine interlocked her fingers with his. "You need to rest," she whispered. Her hand was warm and comforting, like

37

a campfire burning in the cold wilderness. Her presence made him feel more at ease. Her lips parted and from them outpoured a soothing song. The words swaddled him like a cloth as she sang.

> *Beyond the Frosty Peaks so far*
> *Lies the truth of who we are*
> *And how the icy winds recall*
> *The lost tale forgotten by all*
> *On deaf ears, they do fall*
> *Fall into darkness over the years*
> *Causing us to fear what lies beyond*
> *Beyond the Frosty Peaks so far*

She pulled his hand toward her face, his knuckles grazing every pore on her cheek. The bags under his eyes weighed the lids down until they closed, sending him into a deep slumber. In the darkness of sleep, it was not Vargo that awaited him but Mary Katherine, shining brilliantly like the sun.

4

A cool breeze whipped across Gwen's face as she rode next to
the strange man in his chariot. She had seen similar ones before,
but they were kept in better condition and owned by the
wealthiest of nobles. It was rare to meet a man who barely had
a copper to his name possessing one even in shambles such as
this. He drove with one arm extended over the wheel in an aloof
manner. His tunic hung loose, revealing his thin figure and bare
chest. The bucket-shaped hat on his head covered his eyes, and
a dingy pair of sandals wrapped around his feet. He looked like
a beggar that would peddle the streets for coin and spoke few
words. Not even a name was offered. The sun dipped behind the
horizon as the day neared its end, and Gwen grew tired looking
at the same empty, brown terrain.

"How much further?" she asked.

"Not much," the man said, keeping his eyes forward.

Gwen scrunched her cheek against her fist as she watched the landscape glide past them. It was dull and dreary. The only thing that caught her attention was the pastel of colors smeared across the sky. She thought about the various places throughout the continent described in books: the grass-filled hills and plains beyond the Gate to the West; the lush green forests to the north; snow-covered peaks towering over the south; the scenic view of the archipelago off the shores of Papuri; and the blessed city of Illios, which she remembered little about having last visited it as a young girl. A light tap on her shoulder stirred her from her daydream. The man pointed toward a modest skyline of a town and the reflection of the twilight in a sizable lake. The Stagnant Gorge was the name she recalled from readings. It was a strange body of water that had no reason to exist in such a remote area.

Entering the town, they witnessed various merchants sell goods to passersby and a group of children release lanterns into the air, which floated high above the lake, adding their light among the emerging stars. Straggling fishermen docked their boats and hauled in the day's catch.

The chariot came to an abrupt halt as the man turned to her with an outstretched hand. "This is Lundur. That's as far as I said I'd take you."

"So it is." She pulled out her purse and poured fifteen silver coins into his palm. He shoved them into a nearby compartment in the chariot as she stumbled out. She turned to thank him, but he disappeared in a trail of black smoke. There was little else to expect from a man who only agreed to help after his own life was in danger.

Glancing about the bustling town, Gwen found herself at a loss of what to do. The growl of her stomach led her in the direction of a food market. One of the merchants sold grilled fish on a stick. Its charred smell caused her mouth to salivate. Tearing into the white meat, a delectable, sweet taste laced her tongue. The flavor tickled her taste buds and enticed her to ravage the meat until only the stick remained.

No longer distracted by hunger, she explored more of the town. Painters, tailors, and jewelers displayed their finest works, hoping to sell them for a fair price. Sailors and fishermen gathered around a tavern, singing songs that ranged from profane acts of drunken revelry to beautiful ballads of lost love. A young man tinkered with a small mechanical device. It was a copper shell in the shape of a butterfly with its back folded open. She watched him delicately work until the cogs churned and the springs tightened, causing the metal wings to flap. While lacking the grandeur found throughout the capital, Gwen enjoyed observing it all. It was different, and that's what she was looking for.

As time passed and the moon chilled the midnight air, it soon became evident she needed to find somewhere to stay for the night. The tavern closed, sending the sailors home, and the merchants did the same. Gwen never realized how far the temperature had dropped. The breeze cut through her silk cloak, covering her body in goosebumps. Crossing the shoreline, she stumbled upon a black tent faintly outlined in the dancing light of a fire. Desperate for warmth, she approached, hovering her hands over the flames. The heat melted the bumps on her skin and relaxed the tension in her body.

Suddenly, a wild-looking man with rugged features wearing black furs emerged from the tent. Through his matted hair, Gwen noticed a scar across his left cheek. His intense gaze trapped her where she stood as if an arrow caught her foot.

"Who are you?" he growled. "What are you doing snooping around my campsite?"

Gwen searched for an explanation. She desperately wanted to say something to keep the man from hurting her, but not a single word escaped her lips.

"Well?" he said.

Silence still plagued her as she remained frozen in fear.

He lowered himself so his gaze met hers. His auburn eyes reflected the flames of the fire, mimicking its warm hue. "Spit it out, woman. What do you want?"

Closer to the firelight, Gwen noticed a tattoo on his forearm. It was a dagger with runic symbols inscribed on the blade. A mark worn by those of the Hunters' Core. "You're a hunter," she said.

"What gave it away? The scar or the branding? Now, tell me what you're doing around my campsite. Looking to hire my services?"

"No. It was just cold, and I saw the fire, and I'm looking for a place to stay for the night. I only arrived a few hours ago and am new to the town…" Her voice wandered into incoherent rambling.

"Alright, alright," he said, raising a hand for her to stop. "Don't need you to spin me a tale. The Seaside Cottage serves as the usual watering hole for most travelers. Follow the coast in that direction. You can't miss it." Motioning toward the shoreline, he noted her embroidered silk cloak. "If you don't mind me asking, what's a fancy lady like yourself doing out here at this hour all by your lonesome?"

Gwen averted her gaze from his. "As I said, I'm new to town and looking for a place to stay the night."

His eyes narrowed, and his brow twitched. "If you say so." He brushed off his pants as he stood. "It can be dangerous to walk around alone at night. I can act as your escort. At least give me something to do than sit here and stare at the empty water."

Gwen stared at the man blankly, remaining by the fire.

"There's no need to worry, miss," he sighed. "I'm not going to harm you in any way. We kill monsters, not people."

Gwen rose to her feet and, while keeping some distance, followed the hunter down the shoreline. The water of the lake rolled onto the sand, stopping just short of the hunter's path. Gwen lightly kicked sand as she walked. They traveled in silence, and she grew bored thinking back to her journey with the stranger who brought her here.

"Being a hunter," she said, turning to the man in black, "I'm sure you've seen a bit of the continent."

"I've made my way around the east," he said. "Never been beyond the Blade's Trench. Although, I've heard it's a sight to behold."

"I've read the estuaries are as clear as glass. You can see the seafloor from the water's surface." Ever since reading Patterson's *Beyond the Western Gate*, Gwen dreamed of one day swimming in those waters.

"I met a hunter who killed a bolgia out there once. He told me it drowned people in its depths." Swimming in the estuaries suddenly seemed much less appealing. Dead bodies sunken to the bottom, staring with blank, bloated expressions filled her mind. He reassured her that bolgias couldn't reproduce, but it didn't really put her mind at ease.

They arrived at a crooked structure, leaning to one side with warm, inviting lights shining through the windows. Over the entrance hung an old, wooden sign with faded letters spelling *The Seaside Cottage*.

"I trust you can get a room," said the hunter.

"Yes," Gwen replied. She dug out a silver coin from her purse and flipped it to him. Members of the Core rarely did anything without a form of compensation.

Taking it, he smirked. "Appreciated. Before we part, mind telling me your name?"

"Most people call me Gwen," she said.

"Good luck on your journey, Gwen. Ever run into a hunter

this side of the Trench, just mention the name Johnny." With a nod, he headed back down the shoreline toward his camp.

Entering the cottage, a young freckled face woman about Gwen's age stood behind the counter. In the room behind her, a drunken crowd roared with laughter near the bar.

"Need a place to stay?" the attendant asked.

"Yes," said Gwen.

"How long do you plan on staying?"

"I'm not entirely sure yet." Gwen glanced over the woman's shoulder at the commotion. Whatever was taking place must have been a spectacle.

"That's fine." The woman gestured to a large book with a long list of names scrawled along the length of its yellow, aged pages. "Price is ten copper a night. So as long as you can pay, you can stay. Just sign your name and day."

Handing over the copper coins, Gwen signed only her first name along with the day's number in the year. She yearned for a night's rest on a comfy bed.

"Forgive the noise if you could," said the attendant. "Man came in earlier with a handful of silver, challenging anyone to outdrink him."

It couldn't be. Pushing her way through the cheering crowd of drunks, she caught sight of two men sitting across from each other at a table. One was a sailor with a chin strap beard so drunk he struggled to pour his next drink. Across from him, composed and sober, was the stranger she met back at the capital still wearing his bucket-shaped hat. With glasses full, they toasted and slammed their drinks back. The sailor fell backwards out of his chair, spilling most of the liquor onto the floor. The strange man gently placed his empty glass back on the table, wiping his mouth. Cheers erupted as some of the spectators hauled the blacked-out fool away. Money exchanged hands throughout the crowd, some making its way to her beggar-looking travel companion.

As people dispersed, Gwen approached him with her arms crossed and spoke in a condescending tone. "You seem to be enjoying yourself."

"What man wouldn't with fifteen silver?" He didn't seem the least bit caught off guard by her presence. He took a long swig from the bottle he used to refill his glass. "Looking to try your chances at outdrinking me? You'll have quite the advantage, I swear it."

"I have no interest in making a fool of myself," said Gwen.

"Then leave me alone." Shoving her aside, he made his way to the bar. "You've caused me enough trouble already."

She stubbornly followed, sitting next to him. "It was rude to leave me stranded on the street as you did, and you need to work on your social skills. Half a day of travel and not a single word of conversation shared."

"I don't care if I came off as rude." His cheeks reddened from alcohol consumption, but he didn't seem drunk. Hunched over the bar, he continued to down the bottle as if it were water. "We merely partook in a transaction of business. I get you to Lundur, you pay me fifteen silver. That's all there was to it."

"Drink, ma'am?" asked the bartender, a portly man with a few missing teeth.

"Wine, please," said Gwen. The bartender opened an unlabeled bottle of red wine and poured her a glass.

The man sighed, taking another swig from his own bottle. "I really hoped you'd straggle your way into becoming someone else's problem."

She shot him a sideways glance. "Don't go around blaming me for your predicament. I didn't ask you to fight all those thugs."

He chuckled. "Right. So, you would've been fine with them stripping you of your fine garments and coin and doing Emperor knows what else to you?"

She sipped her wine in contempt. After a long day, she found the fruity taste and aroma refreshing. Setting the glass down, her hazel eyes narrowed, turning back toward the stranger. "Where'd you learn to fight like that anyway?" Taking down a group of mercenaries so effortlessly was difficult even for a standard Militia soldier.

"Self-taught mostly. Growing up in the slums, you learn at a young age to defend yourself. If you plan on venturing out to see the world, I'd suggest you do as well."

She studied him head to toe. While skulking about as a pathetic drunk, there was more to this man than her eyes could discern. "Do you have REV implants?"

He turned toward her with a sardonic expression. "Only toxins I pump into my body is this shit." He raised the bottle of liquor in his hand with less than a fourth of its contents still remaining. "If I'm going to poison myself, I at least want to get a good buzz out of it."

Gwen downed the rest of her wine, not realizing how parched she truly was. The bartender refilled her glass. "Why did you help me back there? You said yourself crossing any of the three guilds earns a bounty on your head. It's why you didn't pick a fight with them after they humiliated you."

He didn't say anything, instead opting to drink.

She flashed him a sensual smile and ran a playful hand through her long hair. "Have a thing for distressing damsels? I noticed the way you gawked at me as we left the capital when my hood fell." He didn't respond, brooding over the bar. She found it amusing to tease him.

The wine continued to flow as Gwen pestered him further. She considered it penance for his lack of conversation during their prior trip. Since he didn't entertain her then, he would make up for it now. Soon, her head grew light and face numb. The bartender poured the last bit of wine from the unlabeled bottle. She was never much of a drinker and never finished an entire bottle by herself. Her vision blurred, and the room spun. Her body tipped over in the seat and fell to the floor. The last thing she saw before blacking out was the beggar-looking man reach out to catch her.

5

Remnants of the fire still haunted the halls of the north end of the palace as the smell of smoke and soot permeated the air. The dim light of a torch guided Blackwood in his march forward. He felt rejuvenated after the short rest in Mary Katherine's comfort. Passing the Great Hall, he could still hear the distant screams of those fleeing in terror from the flames and sellswords. It didn't take him long to reach the hallway housing the entrance to the Tomb. Standing beside the iron door were Rahm and Captain Ben Green, a sturdy man and second-division captain of the Phoenix Militia. His spikey hair stuck out of his head like golden cactus needles. He held a torch in his left hand, and in his right was his infamous mace, known to crush a man's skull in a single swing.

Blackwood greeted them upon his approach, "Ambassador. Captain."

"You seem to have regained a spring in your step," said

Rahm. "Though you still look worse for wear."

"Never mind my appearance." He motioned to the door. "Shall we?"

Captain Green led the way down the spiral staircase. The nine stone thrones awaited them in the chamber. They traced the edges of the room using the light of their torches to unveil any hidden passages. Blackwood stumbled upon a grate in the floor at the far corner of the room. Beckoning the other two over, he bent down to observe it. Through the grating, he could see a hole large enough for a man to fit through, but bars thick with steel barricaded it. Grabbing hold of the grate, he tried to lift it, but to no avail. It proved too heavy for a normal person to budge.

"Allow me, Chancellor," said the Militia captain. With one arm, he peeled the grating back, uncovering the hole.

Blackwood tossed his torch into the pit. The flame descended about twelve feet before hitting solid ground.

Rahm gestured toward the hole. "After you, Blackwood."

Blackwood unhooked the pin clasping his cape to his shoulders, and lowered himself into the pit using the rocks jutting from the wall. Reaching the bottom, he picked up the torch and found himself at the entrance of a tunnel. Rahm followed him, almost slipping off the rocks as he climbed down. Captain Green was the last to descend. He jumped in as the metal grate slammed shut behind him with a piercing ring. Together, they marched in single file through the cavern. The ceiling was eight feet tall, enough for Blackwood to proceed without ducking his head. Darkness swelled around them, kept at bay by the light of their torches. The silence was deafening as every subtle noise seemed amplified, from the crackling flames to their shuffling footsteps. A pile of rocks blocked a branching pathway, forcing them to continue down the main route. Deeper and deeper, they traveled. It seemed endless.

"This passageway has remained open so far," said Rahm. He trailed from the back of their line as Captain Green forged ahead at the front.

"Indeed, it has," echoed Blackwood.

"I did not inquire back at your office, but I'm sure you have some sneaking suspicions about the identity of the perpetrators."

"Everyone has suspicions." Blackwood leered over his shoulder, aware of the conversation's direction.

"True, but certain suspicions weigh heavier than others." He clasped a meaty hand on Blackwood's shoulder, stopping him for a moment. "I know you're not a fool. You understand as well as I that if Vargo did use the mines, then someone well versed in the kingdom's history put him up to this plot. Someone who knew in a moment of crisis you and the king would be stowed away in the Tomb. Someone who once served under Parliament."

Rahm despised the rebels more than anyone. He held onto the ideals passed down from the era of King Peter's father that those who oppose the crown or its justice should be crushed. It would be a lie for Blackwood to deny his lingering suspicion that the rebels, or at least Elliot Durham, had a hand in this affair. Making such a claim, however, would most likely reignite the war between them.

Blackwood brushed Rahm's hand from his shoulder. "Suspicions are just that without proper proof, which you'll need to convince the king to abandon the peace he's long awaited."

"I understand it's not my place to speak on political matters," said Green, "but this peace you claim to establish has only set a precedent." Having noticed Blackwood and Rahm pause, he stopped as well. The harsh shadows of the torch flames cast the far side of his face in ominous shadows. "It's informed others who may wish to oppose the kingdom that if they push hard enough, we will relent. When a platoon of troops mutinies against their superior officer, do we forgive and allow them to go their merry way? No. We disband the platoon and punish those involved appropriately. Otherwise, we'd have mutinies popping up like weeds."

Blackwood glared at the captain in an ugly pause. "As you said, it's not your place to speak on political matters."

They ushered further into the tunnel, finally reaching a faint glow accompanied by the roar of the sea. Stepping through, the three men found themselves on a cliff overlooking the torrential, blue waters. Across the way was a small section of the city lining the rest of the coastline. Blackwood could hardly believe it. One of the mining tunnels managed to survive and it led directly into the Tomb.

"Emperor be praised," said Rahm. He turned to Blackwood with a sneer. "Suspicions can sometimes be correct."

The hour of their return was late in the night. Blackwood clasped his cape over his shoulders as Rahm climbed out of the pit with Captain Green's assistance. One mystery was solved, but the question of who hired the assassin still remained. Although Elliot was a prime suspect, Blackwood could not decipher how he discovered the entrance to formulate such a plan. Leaving the Tomb and heading back to their chambers, a panicked, young servant crossed their path.

He addressed them with a bow, "Chancellor Blackwood. Ambassador Krawczyk. The king has requested your presence in the throne room immediately."

Blackwood and Rahm looked at each other in bewilderment. It was strange for the king to summon anyone at such an ungodly hour. They raced through the halls toward the throne room where Peter sat in the ivory throne atop a mountain of stairs. Wings of creamy white thorns crafted from the tusks of creatures long extinct extended from the king's back. Leaned forward, he met them with a dreadful glare. Mary Katherine rested at the foot of the staircase as if she'd been waiting for some time.

Blackwood spoke through panting breaths, "Forgive our tardiness, Your Majesty. We were preoccupied with—"

"No need to explain yourselves," said Peter in a low rumble. "We have a dire situation on our hands that needs immediate attention." The seriousness of his tone and brooding demeanor cloaked him in the shadow of his father. This was not his friend Peter they were speaking to. This was King Clougher. The three members of Parliament were brought to one knee, listening intently. "My daughter, Guinevere, has gone missing. I want searches conducted for her promptly before it's too late." Blackwood's heart sank to the pit of his stomach.

Mary Katherine shot to her feet. "What do you mean, she's gone missing? She just disappeared, and no one noticed until now?"

Blackwood grabbed her arm in an attempt to lower her back down, but she didn't budge.

"I echo your concerns and frustrations," replied the king. Standing from the throne, he descended the stairway in a melancholic fashion. "Which is why I want the situation rectified quickly. Ambassador Krawczyk, command Captain Green to dispatch his forces and comb your division by the morn. Send word to Fletcher to do the same. Ambassador Brown, have soldiers search the city in case she's still here. Blackwood, keep an ear open in the underground. This matter is to remain confidential for the time being. We still don't know the identities of Vargo's proprietors, and if they don't know this information already, then it should be kept that way."

Blackwood and Rahm bowed their heads, speaking in

harmony, "Yes, Your Majesty." Mary Katherine ripped her hand away from Blackwood's, storming out of the throne room. The chancellor fought the urge to chase her and instead lingered with Rahm. Peter noticed something troubled them as they remained glued to the tiled floors.

"Something on your minds?" he asked.

Rahm cleared his throat. "My King, the chancellor and I have recently discovered that one of the ancient mining tunnels remains open, and we believe it to be the assassin's method infiltrating the palace."

Peter looked to Blackwood. "Is this true?"

"Yes," said the chancellor. "We've witnessed it with our own eyes."

The king nodded stiffly. "Only someone close to the crown could have that knowledge. Continue your investigation, but my daughter's safety takes priority."

"Of course," said Blackwood.

The two men bowed and dismissed themselves. They ventured through the halls, hurrying to complete their commands.

"Quite rude for the ambassador to storm out like she did," Rahm commented. "It's apparent she favors the girls, but there's no need to overreact. It's unbecoming for a member of Parliament."

Blackwood glared at the hefty man. "These are stressful times, easy to be overcome with emotion."

"It is not our duty to act on emotion. Sound minds are needed in stressful situations." He gave a mocking glance in Blackwood's direction. "Perhaps a good lay might relieve some of her stress."

Blackwood shoved him into the wall, an arm pressed against his thick neck. The ambassador squirmed like a pig, clawing at Blackwood. All that weight offered little strength. The pudgy man gasped for air as the chancellor held firm.

"Careful how you speak," Blackwood threatened through gritted teeth. "Just because you helped me in my investigation does not make us jovial companions."

"Is there a problem?" boomed a voice down the hall. Captain Green stood there, mace in hand. His olive gaze was similar to the eye of a great storm, calm for the time being.

Blackwood released the ambassador and stepped away.

"Not to worry, Captain," said Rahm, casually brushing himself off. "The chancellor and I were butting heads as usual. Now, if you'll excuse me, I have a message to deliver to Ambassador Fletcher." He strutted off, a smug expression smeared over his face. Captain Green lingered for a moment, tapping the gnarled end of his mace against this shoulder. He then followed the ambassador.

Blackwood remained in the hall. He sympathized with Mary Katherine's pain. She cared for the king's daughters like they were her own. If anyone had a right to snap at Peter, it was her. Wading through the palace, he ventured to her chambers. His hand hovered over the door, tempted to knock, but he restrained himself. Tonight, she needed to be alone. He had no words of comfort to offer, not yet. For now, the best thing he could do was find the princess.

6

A bloom of orange light splashed across the sky, penetrating the window and stinging Anden's eyes. If only he'd gotten any sleep. Instead, he found himself setting a glass of water on the bedside table of the passed-out noblewoman. Sprawled out in a drunken stupor, the maroon cloak unraveled a white dress wrapped around an hourglass figure. She was a sight to behold, and that's all Anden was content in doing. He was too tired and sober for any lecherous temptations to cloud his judgment. Of all the places and people, why him? He should have left town as soon as he dropped her off, but the long day's travel and jingle of the newly acquired silver persuaded him otherwise. He should have ignored her at the bar or just retired to his room. Even now, it was in his best interest to disappear and never see her again. She was a dangerous person for someone like him to be around, but after years of monotony in laying low, that danger bred a hint of excitement.

He drowned that thought with a swig of his flask. He needed to rest and head westward. The silver in his pocket alleviated many challenges from finding a new city to hide and avoid the Militia in. The decision was simple. Exiting the room, he heard a chatter of voices from below. Leaning over the railing, he saw a handful of Militia soldiers talking to the young attendant. She pointed up a floor in Anden's direction, and the men marched up the stairs. Anden lowered his hat, obscuring his face, and strolled the other way.

The stampede of boots hammered against the stairs as they hurried to the entrance of the noblewoman's room. It wasn't uncommon for the Militia to aid in searching for a missing member of the nobility, but to assemble one within a day was strange. Anden heard one of the soldiers kick the door in, followed by a fearful shriek. The woman continued to yell as they stormed the room, and Anden kept walking. It wasn't his business to get involved with, that was until the distinct chime of clinking shackles caught his ear. The woman's screams became muffled. Something was wrong. Against his better judgment, Anden turned around and added a drunken wobble to his stride. Approaching the room, he leaned onto the frame of the doorway. The woman was gagged with a cloth and held down on the bed by three soldiers. One of them held shackles in his hands, preparing to clasp them around the woman's wrists. She looked at Anden, desperation in her eyes.

"Sorry, gents," Anden said with a slur. "Must have the wrong room."

One of them turned around with a hand on the hilt of his blade. "Got that right. Now piss off."

Anden faked a belch. "I'm not one to judge, but I didn't know they allowed that in this establishment."

The soldier drew his sword. "If you don't piss off, I'll arrest you for obstruction of the king's justice." Anden continued to sway in the doorway, giggling. The soldier marched toward him, sword poised to strike. Anden caught his arm, bent the man over his knee, and struck the back of his nape. The Militia soldier's body went limp and dropped to the floor. The one holding shackles drew his blade as well and charged, swinging. Anden dodged his slashes and, grabbing a candlestick, struck the second soldier on the side of the head. Blood trickled down his face as he, too, fell to the ground. The third soldier unsheathed a knife and pinned Anden against the wall. The tip of the blade hovered inches away from Anden's neck as he held the man at bay. The soldier forced all his weight into the knife to pierce Anden's flesh. Anden kicked the soldier in the groin, causing him to collapse, and knocked him unconscious with another strike. Commotion spread throughout the rest of the cottage. Anden slammed the door shut and barricaded it with whatever furniture he could find.

The woman pulled the cloth from her mouth. "What's going on? Those soldiers gagged me and tried to put me in shackles."

"I'm not sure," said Anden, "but we need to get out of here."

Checking that his barricade was secure, he tore open the window. They were two stories up—an easy enough jump. Scooping the woman up, he perched himself on the windowsill. Pounding erupted against the door with muffled shouts. "Just hold on and don't squirm too much."

Pushing off from the ledge, the woman locked her arms around his neck, screaming the entire way. Landing on both feet, Anden rounded the corner of the cottage where he left his functional pile of scraps. Tossing the woman into the back, he vaulted into the driver's seat. The machine groaned as he pulled the levers and pushed the pedals, desperate to get the engine kicking.

The noise summoned more Militia soldiers as they rounded the inn, sprinting toward them. Anden adjusted one of the levers on the wheel until the groan erupted into a roar. Slamming his foot onto one of the pedals, the chariot raced down the street. Townsfolk dove out of their path, forcing Anden to swerve. A two-horse carriage followed behind them, with one soldier reining the horses and the other steadying a rifle. Anden glanced back in time to see the woman poke her head up from the back seat. As he shoved her back down, the rifle flashed with a cloud of smoke, sending a bullet whizzing by overhead. The protective glass in the front shattered into a spiderweb of cracks as the bullet pierced it. Reaching the outskirts of Lundur, Anden adjusted the lever once more and slid his foot onto another pedal. The machine roared louder and surged ahead at an increased speed, leaving their pursuers in a fog of black smoke.

The old clunker sputtered down the dusty countryside before coming to a complete stop. It had been a while since Anden pushed the old girl to her limits. A miracle it managed to remain in one piece. The woman curled up in the back mumbled to herself.

"They shot me," she said. "I can't believe they shot at me."

Anden twisted himself around. "You a thief or something?"

There was a fearful silence as the woman rocked back and forth in shock.

"Those soldiers were about to arrest you if I hadn't stopped them," said Anden. "So, how about you tell me who you are?"

"I'm not a thief," she said, averting her eyes.

"Yeah, sure. Doesn't change the fact the Militia apparently wants your head. Now, tell me who you are, so I know what I'm dealing with here."

She heaved out a sigh. "My name is Guinevere Clougher, first daughter of King Peter Clougher and heir to the throne." She stared at him with an expectant gaze.

He buried his blank expression into the palm of his hand. Pulling out his flask, he took a long pull. "Unbelievable." He cast his attention to the sky as if speaking to a higher power. "After all this time, it comes crashing down like an avalanche."

Climbing out of his seat, he opened the front of the chariot where the engine resided. A billow of steam wafted into the air as the metal held a faint, red glow.

The princess poked her head out over the side. "What will you do with me?" she asked.

"I'm not entirely sure." He fanned the steam with his hat. "Can't take you back to Alastair, not if the Militia is already trying to track you down, and I'll most likely end up getting arrested. I could leave you behind somewhere. That would be *my* best option." He looked at her with a facetious grin. "But maybe I do have a thing for distressing damsels." The glow of the metal died, and the steam faded. "There is a place we can go to catch our breath and think things over." He closed the hood of the chariot and climbed back into the driver's seat. Revving it to life, they took off across the countryside.

"If we're continuing to travel together, I would like to know your name," said the princess.

"Anden," he said.

"Okay, Anden. Where is this place you're taking us?"

"Sandur," he replied. "To see an old friend."

7

Nothing in the world bored Reed more than listening to her generals bicker. Under her uncle, they acted like trained dogs heeding his every word. With her, they barked at each other like strays until she tugged on their leash. Her high overseer, Elliot Durham, was meant to assist in bringing them to heel but ended up no different than the others. No wonder her uncle entrusted her to lead the rebellion once he died. He recognized they were nothing but fools wanting more of the same except to be in higher positions of power. Unfortunately for them, they won't be the ones to gain more power at the conclusion of the war. Once the royal family is overthrown, and Parliament eradicated, power will be given to the people to elect their own officials in their own council. No longer would corrupt politicians manipulate the system to benefit themselves and the nobles who filled their pockets with coin at the expense of everyone else.

Elliot tapped a finger on the table, signaling for her to

intervene. Cornelius Riggs currently bit at the throat of Sean Watts, their master engineer, about their next course of action.

"The king's no fool," said Cornelius. "Unleashing your contraption recklessly could cost us our trump card."

"And what will the Militia do?" Watts asked, gesturing with his arms. "With my creation, we can easily breach the capital's walls and lay siege to the city. Within a day, we can level the palace to rubble."

"A siege could last days, maybe a week—more than enough time for Green and Balavan to rally reinforcements. If we're going to strike, it needs to be quick and when they're caught off guard. His daughter's coronation would have been perfect if things had gone as planned. It might be best to play out this truce and wait for the king to die. He's old enough."

Watts rose from his seat, standing above the other generals. "We've been waiting for the past decade. My machine will not sit here and collect dust while the Militia continues to bolster its forces."

Reed silenced them. "Don't get too anxious, Watts. Your machine still needs to be properly tested before we prepare an attack." The strength of her emerald gaze forced the engineer back into his seat. They enlisted the help of many tinkerers, some more skilled than others to construct his monstrosity. It was a challenge taking many years to complete and more so to keep secret from the kingdom. "Cornelius is right. We do not want to play our hand earlier than needed. Adjustments to the plan will be made. Our opportunity to deal a fatal strike will soon come."

The war tent's entrance folded open as the hooded visage of Vargo Vasallo stepped inside. The assassin casually seated himself at the far end of the table, opposite Reed. The two generals closest to him subtly shifted themselves further away.

"You certainly took your time getting here," said Reed. She'd summoned him days ago but never heard back.

"Excuse my tardiness," he hissed. His white eyes glossed over the map spreading the length of the table. "I had other business to attend to."

"Afraid to face your failure, I'm sure," chided Elliot. Her high overseer distrusted any hired sword. He assured them their allegiance would flip like a coin tossed by the highest bidder. Usually, his words held true, but something was different about Vargo. After all, he sought them out, somehow vaguely aware of their plans.

The assassin held up his arms as if caught in some criminal act. "Not my brightest moment, I admit. Old he may be, but the king still moves swiftly and knows when to strike. Captain Gunnway was a small problem as well."

"The fact remains that the king and chancellor's heads still rest on their shoulders," said Reed, crossing her legs. "So, you will not be receiving the other half of your promised payment."

"That's fair business." Vargo leaned over the table, casting an ominous shadow over the map. His rotten, yellow teeth peeked out from his hood. "However, I might possess some information you may find quite valuable."

Reed's lips tightened. "How valuable do you estimate it to be?"

"I'll say a quarter of my original payment."

Elliot leaned over to whisper. "It's a sham. What information could he have that we don't? He's only looking to scrape up any extra coin he can."

Reed pondered the assassin's offer. While being a sellsword and hired killer, he wasn't the type of man to con people out of their coin. He possessed too much pride for that. If he claimed to have valuable information, then it must be true.

"Deal," she said, ignoring Elliot's disapproving glare.

Vargo emitted a cruel cackle. All the generals at the table grew tense as if a chilling breeze blew through the tent. "Whispers claim that the king's eldest daughter has gone missing from the palace and Militia soldiers have already been sent out in search of her. No doubt their forces will spread thin in the coming days the longer she remains unfound. A useful distraction, wouldn't you agree?"

The generals murmured amongst themselves.

"Where did you come by such information?" Elliot asked.

"I have connections who possess a reliable network of informants across the continent." Vargo leaned back in his chair, crossing his legs as if to mirror Reed. "Very reliable."

"We should check the validity of this claim," whispered

Elliot.

Reed tried to read the assassin, but his foggy eyes obscured his thoughts. "Collect your payment outside," she said with contempt. "Don't travel too far. If your information proves to be true, we'll be in need of your services again."

Vargo rose from his seat, the assortment of daggers clanging. "As long as I get paid," he said before sauntering out of the tent. He left them all in a chilling silence.

Reed broke it with a commanding voice, "General Watts, if your engineer's reports are true, your contraption should be prepared for a test?"

A grin crept across Watts' face. "Yes, ma'am. I've inspected nearly every inch myself."

"Then pray that it should pass with flying colors. Our opportunity to strike may still come."

Watts glanced over at Cornelius' sour expression.

"That is all." She nodded them out.

While her generals shuffled out of the tent, Elliot remained with Reed, visibly disturbed. "It's foolish to trust that man more than we already have."

Reed poured herself a glass of red Sanduran wine. "Because he's a sellsword?"

"Not just any sellsword," Elliot spat. "He's the man who killed your father years ago. Doesn't it seem odd to have him working for us? Who's to say he won't turn around and slit your throat?"

Reed sipped her wine. Strutting behind Elliot's chair, she dragged her fingers across his shoulders. "Let's not forget, you once served as an ambassador for Parliament at that same time. Are you suggesting that you also shouldn't be trusted?" Elliot stammered to defend himself, but she cut him off. "Vargo is merely a tool. It's not him I don't trust. It's others who could have him under their employ."

"So," Elliot said, "if his word holds its weight, what are your plans?"

Reed swirled the glass in her hand. The red liquid churned, creating a small vortex. "We'll use this opportunity to strike. First by crippling the Militia, then attacking the capital. In the meantime, I want a spy tailing Vargo. See if we can find out who these connections are that can gather such delicate information."

Elliot rose from his seat and took his leave. Reed lounged in her chair, enjoying the wine. She studied the map laid out before her, scanning from the western estuaries to the city of Alastair. While not exactly according to plan, things seemed to be working out in their favor all the same. Other players may be afoot hatching their own schemes, but the kingdom remained her greatest obstacle. She wouldn't rest until the blood of the royal family nourished the soil.

8

The sun drifted across its apex in the sky, and the heat forced Gwen to remove her silk cloak as sweat drenched her body and stained her white dress. Her hangover from the previous night tied her stomach in a knot and drove a nail into her temple. She laid fetal in the backseat, arms wrapped around herself, hoping for the condition to subside. Anden wasn't faring much better as his eyes closed every so often only to jerk himself awake after his head started to drift. The chariot traveled at a slower pace than before. Whatever Anden did to ensure their escape in Lundur seemed to damage the machine in some way.

"Do we have any water?" she asked. Her throat was dry, and her lips started to crack. Anden handed her his flask. She shoved it away. "I said water. Is booze all you ever drink?"

"Pretty much," he said, taking a swig.

Gwen shook her head in disgust. "No one can survive like that. How are you not constantly drunk?"

"How do you know I'm not?"

Gwen turned over, facing the back of her seat. She was in no mood to deal with his snarky remarks. The chariot sputtered to a crawl before stopping completely.

"Of all the times," Anden muttered under his breath. Climbing out of his seat, he rounded toward the back and opened a compartment.

"Is something wrong again?" Gwen asked, poking her head up over the seat.

"No," said Anden. "Just needs a little fuel, is all." He removed a rusted container with liquid slushing around inside. Gripping the front seat cushion and hoisting it up, he poured the container's contents into a sizable copper tank. Gwen recognized the scent of the liquid. It held a sweet chemical odor that tickled her nose in a strange, satisfying way.

"That's gasoline," she said. Years ago, a pair of nobles presented the substance to her father and Blackwood, explaining its properties and capabilities. Its aroma filled the throne room.

"That it is." Anden finished filling the tank. "Going to need to get some more soon." He returned the container to the back compartment of the chariot and mounted his seat at the wheel. Refueled, he reignited the engine, and they continued their journey.

After spending a long day in the sweltering heat, Gwen's hangover finally passed. Shadows from a nearby rock formation stretched across the land. Anden maneuvered the chariot under an archway and silenced its low hum.

Rubbing her eyes, Gwen glanced around, seeing nothing but the same dreary landscape and a jagged slab of earth erected toward the heavens. "Why are we stopping? This can't be the place."

Anden leaned back in his seat, tilting his hat further over his face. "I haven't gotten a wink for almost a whole day. I need to rest my eyes for a moment, unless you want to end up in a nasty crash. It's just for a few minutes."

Seeing no point in arguing, Gwen lay flat on the seat, staring up into the gradient-colored sky as a chill breeze cooled her tender, burnt skin. It wasn't long before boredom seeped in, and since her legs felt stiff, she decided to go for a walk. Stepping out of the chariot, her chest pushed forward, forcing her body into a prolonged and euphoric stretch. She strolled along the base of the archway. A few pebbles and rocks scattered the ground. Picking them up, she flung them toward the horizon, trying to throw each one further than the last. The game entertained her until the sun vanished, and it grew too dark to see the rocks land. Assuming enough time had passed for Anden to rest, she headed back to the chariot to wake him. Rounding the formation, her foot caught on something and sent her face-first into the dirt. Looking over her shoulder, Gwen's eyes widened in horror.

A thin, bony hand as pale as moonlight stuck out of the ground, twitching. Gwen lay there, paralyzed with fear while its sharp, claw-like nails dug into the earth. A gaunt creature with rags of skin hanging from its bones emerged from the crumbling dirt. Black voids, darker than the night sky, stared at her with rows of jagged teeth coated in a thick syrup of saliva. It stared at her with an unyielding hunger. She tried to crawl away, but the creature gripped a talon around her ankle. Its icy touch burned her skin, and she unleashed an ear-piercing scream. Writhing on the ground, she thrashed her legs in an attempt to escape its grasp. The creature held firm, pulling her closer toward its decrepit body, ready to rip her apart.

Gwen gave one last jerk of her trapped leg and found that it came free. Crawling away, she could still feel the cold, burning sensation against her skin. The clawed hand still gripped tightly around her ankle, but it had been severed from the rest of the creature. A metal rod slammed into the monster's head, ripping it from its neck and killing it. Anden stood over its limp body wielding a weapon she had never seen before. It consisted of three metal rods linked by a series of chains.

"Get to the carriage, now," he demanded.

A horde of the same creatures rose from the ground, surrounding them. With the arm still attached to her leg, Gwen hurried toward the chariot alongside Anden. The ghastly figures pursued, crawling on all fours as different parts of their body convulsed with each step possessed by a dark, foreign nature. Anden flourished his weapon, swinging with great speed. He cleared a path to the chariot, but the creatures were relentless. Even when losing a limb or cut completely in half, they continued their pursuit until drawing their last breath. Their numbers grew as Gwen launched herself into the backseat and kicked any that tried climbing over the chariot's side. Anden ignited the engine and slammed a foot onto a pedal. The chariot shook as they barreled through the horde. Black blood splattered all around them as they escaped into the night.

Catching her breath and calming her nerves, Gwen pried the severed hand from her ankle. In its place was a patch of discolored skin. "What were those things?"

"Fleshlings," said Anden. "It's said their touch is colder than the highest point of the Frostbitten Peaks. Can't stand the sun's heat, so they come out at night."

Gwen's sister told her of such creatures as children. They were the reason for her mother's death, but she never saw one before, not even a sketch or rendition. All she knew was that they haunted her sister's childhood dreams and sent her into a fit of fearful wails every night.

"Don't they usually stay near the Demons' Cavity?" she asked.

"Usually. It's common for a handful to venture further out, but I've never seen a horde of that size. It's a bad omen."

After riding a bit further, they arrived at a house in the middle of nowhere. Only the glow of the candles in each window penetrated the shroud of night. Anden instructed Gwen to stay close and not speak. Still shaking with fear from the fleshling encounter, she agreed. Five steps after exiting the chariot, they were met with a flash of gunshot and a bullet striking the ground before them. Silhouetted in the candlelight was a man holding a gun.

"Another step, and it's a bullet in your leg." He possessed a deep, booming voice that rumbled the air.

Anden placed his hands on his hips. "After these past few years, you've forgotten what the roar of the old girl sounds like?"

"Roar?" the man said. "Sounds more like a dying croak."

"Yeah. Well, she's taken quite the beating."

Holstering his pistol, the man strutted up to greet them. "Seems you have too. Must be in some deep shit if you've come out here to me."

"It's a long story," said Anden. "For now, we just need a place to stay."

"That I can do." He turned to Gwen. "Who's the lady?"

"She's part of the story. I'll tell you all about it tomorrow."

They followed the man into the house. Under the dim lighting, it was difficult to see any discerning features of his face. All Gwen could gather was that he had a gun and wore a heavy set of boots that pounded against the floorboards. Ascending a staircase, he showed them to their rooms for the night. As soon as Gwen fell onto the bed, the mark on her ankle started to burn again. She had trouble sleeping. The fleshling's black, soulless gaze awaited her each time she closed her eyes. Now she understood the trauma her younger sister faced all those years ago. She understood why the Hunters' Core was a necessary entity on the continent. For the first time, she understood why her father forbade her to leave the capital.

9

Gwen awoke to the call of a rooster. Climbing out of bed, she found a pair of clean clothes folded on the bedside table. She welcomed them as her own dress barely held a white color being covered in a thick coat of dirt and splotches of blood. It had been two days since her last bath, and she wreaked something foul. Grabbing the clothes, she sneaked across the hall to indulge in a relaxing bath. The warm water soothed her skin, washing away the filth and grime that gathered over her travels. Fresh and clean, she donned the new outfit of an orange sundress and blue jacket. It was a more modest style than she was used to, but she liked it. A pair of work boots was provided as well. They were a loose fit, meant for someone with larger-sized feet than herself, but the sandals she originally wore started to chafe her heels.

She clumsily descended the staircase to keep the boots from slipping off her feet with each step. At the base of the stairs, the morning light flooded the windows of what was a dim room in the night. Now, she could see the various knick-knacks and antiques decorating the space. It was almost a bit much as if nothing had ever been tossed away throughout the years of occupation. Searching for anyone who might be awake, she stumbled across a framed painting on the wall. The shapes and colors flowed into each other as if the artist's hand had never lifted from the canvas. Studying it, she made out two blobs to be people, a man and a woman, toiling a field of some kind.

A muffled grunt broke her attention from the painting to a nearby window. Outside, an unfamiliar man heaved a group of barrels into a carriage. Gwen headed out to meet him, the squeak of the door garnering his attention. He greeted her with a toothy grin that contrasted with his dark-toned skin.

"Morning," he said. Gwen recognized the booming voice from the previous night. It was the stranger with the gun. He was quite handsome with a shaved head and a well-groomed beard of black hair. "Good to see the clothes fit. Figured you could use some new threads."

Gwen gave a little twirl. "Yes, thank you. The boots are a bit big."

"Sorry about that." He heaved another barrel onto the carriage. "Ma always preferred her boots on the larger side." Patting his brow dry with a rag, he took her hand. "Wesley's the name. Wesley Sparrow."

"It's a pleasure to meet you," she said. "Call me Gwen. Are you going somewhere?"

"Need to head into to town to drop off some supplies. Anden up yet?"

Gwen glanced back toward the house. "I didn't see him." Her stomach growled. After everything that happened the previous day, she never took the time to eat and an emptiness sat in her gut.

Wesley cracked a smile. "You should join me on my trip, then. I know a good place to grab some breakfast."

After the incident in Lundur, Gwen didn't think it wise to go into town. The last thing she wanted was to run into more Militia soldiers who might put her in shackles, but she was hungry. Wesley eyed her as she rubbed a hand over her arm, taking time to respond.

"There's no need to worry about running into any Militia forces out here," he said, checking the reins on his horses. "Bordering three divisions of the kingdom and not a single one pays any attention to us."

Gwen's eyes widened. "I didn't say anything about—"

"And you didn't need to," said Wesley. "It's been five years since that bastard has shown his face. Only thing that could bring his sorry ass back to my doorstep is trouble with the kingdom's enforcers." He motioned for her to join him on the carriage. "Come on. I'd prefer to have some company during the trip."

Gwen did as he instructed and sat next to him as Wesley gripped the reins. With a sharp flick of his wrists, the horses trotted down a beaten pathway away from the estate. Despite being early, the sun proved to be as brutal as it had the day before. Waves of heat danced across the land, forming puddles of mirages.

"What supplies are you taking into town?" asked Gwen, looking at the barrels bunched together behind them.

"Wine," Wesley replied. "The Sparrow vineyard is one of the few that produces a variation of the famous Sanduran brands and has for many years. I took over after my parents passed away."

"I'm sorry to hear that," said Gwen.

"Don't be. They lived a full life and died when nature deemed it their time. Not many others can say the same." The gaze of his yellow eyes sparkled as it lifted toward the sky. His irises were a reflection of the sun in the spring. "What about yourself? How did you come to be in Anden's company?"

Gwen tightened her lips, choosing her words carefully. "A series of odd and troubling events."

Wesley bellowed a hearty chuckle. "Sounds about right to meet someone like him, but it's good to know he's still kicking." A subtle hint of happiness warmed his face.

They continued in a comforting silence, approaching the town of Sandur, which was small given the vast landscape. Buildings sat side by side, constructed in strips along the roadways. People bustled about, coming and going out of the different buildings. One, in particular, gathered a large crowd, drinking out of tankards, and gorgeous women in corsets eyeing men that walked by. Wesley pulled on the reins for the horses to stop and let Gwen off.

"I've got to attend to my business." He pointed to a small shop with a faint coat of pink paint wedged between two larger structures. "Miss Shelley makes a mean scone at the bakery. Grab something to eat. I'll join you shortly."

Gwen nodded and headed toward the shop while Wesley continued down the road. The scent of fresh flour greeted her upon entering. It was a cozy interior, providing a single table for customers to sit at. No one stood at the counter, which displayed samples of different pastries behind a pane of glass.

"Hello," Gwen called out.

There was a clatter from the back room. A woman stumbled out wearing a dirty apron. She had a motherly look to her, with hair tied in a bun and dimples perfectly pinching her cheeks. Flour caked her hands, having been interrupted from baking.

"Sorry for the inconvenience," she said, wiping her hands clean on her apron. "My daughter is out running errands, so it's just me for the time being. What can I get you?"

"I was hoping to try one of your scones," said Gwen. "Word is they're quite delicious."

"That's too kind," Miss Shelley gushed. Her voice had a drawl to it, stretching out the vowels a bit. "I'll have them out right away."

She disappeared into the back room, leaving Gwen to her own accord. Other than staring at the pastries on display, there was little else offered to preoccupy time. Gwen strode over to the window to observe the activities of the town. A woman in a teal dress carrying a rucksack crossed the street and entered the shop. Seeing Gwen, her eyes widened, and her mouth fell agape.

"Are you looking to order something?" the woman asked. "My apologies, I was out buying ingredients."

"It's okay," Gwen reassured. "Miss Shelley already took my order."

"Good to hear." The woman carried the sack into the backroom. "Mama, here's the stock you needed me to get."

Gwen faintly heard Miss Shelley's voice carry through the doorway. "Thank you, deary. Now, go give our customer some company while she waits."

The woman returned with a smile and cheery attitude. "I don't think I've seen your face around here before. Just passing through?"

"In a way," said Gwen. "Had a run-in with some fleshlings the other night and needed to make a stop."

"Shame to hear. More of those vile things seem to pop up with every passing day. Many of the farmers have had to resort to hiring hunters to guard their fields and cattle. Luckily, none seem to make their way into town." She held out her hand. "I'm Elizabeth, by the way, but you can just call me Liz."

Gwen took it, giving a shake. "Gwen. Nice to meet you."

"So, Gwen," said Liz. "Where are you staying in town?"

Gwen opened her mouth to speak, but the front door suddenly burst open and two men wearing ratty, brown clothing strutted in. One was shorter with an angular face and a plume of orange hair. The other was a hulking mass of muscle with a thick horseshoe mustache. They both sported a red patch sewn into the shoulder of their clothes. A sign they were members of the rebellion. Gwen backed away as they sauntered up to the counter.

Liz's inviting hospitality turned into hostility. "What do you want, Minks?"

The shorter one tossed an arm onto the counter, leaning on it. "I'm here on behalf of Perrotti for his payment." He pulled out a small piece of parchment with writing on it. "Your mother didn't pay last month's tax, so now she owes double."

Liz clenched her jaw. "We just restocked on supplies. We can pay some of it tomorrow with whatever business we get today."

Minks shook his head. "Some isn't going to cut it. You either pay all of it or we'll come up with another way to clear the debt." His eyes traced the subtle curves of her petite frame. His lewd gaze even made Gwen uncomfortable.

"What's going on here, Minks?" Wesley stood in the doorway glaring at the two men.

"If it ain't the golden goose," said Minks. "You just finish shitting your eggs for the boss?"

"You haven't answered my question."

Minks responded with a condescending sneer, "Just talking business." He slid the parchment across the counter to Liz. "Give that to your mother and tell her we'll be back by the evening to collect. Come on, Rory."

The muscled man stared at Gwen for a moment before following Minks out of the shop, shoving their way past Wesley.

"What was all that about?" Wesley asked Liz.

"Nothing beyond their usual thuggish behavior," she said, taking the parchment off the counter.

Miss Shelley exited the backroom with a plate full of fresh scones and handed them to Gwen. "Here you go, deary. I hope you enjoy them." Turning to see Wesley, she gasped in shock, her cheeks reddening. "Oh, Wesley dear. I didn't know you came in. Can I get you anything?"

"No, Miss Shelley. I'm glad to see you cooked up something for my companion."

Liz handed her mother the piece of parchment. Reading it, her face hardened for a moment before returning to a dimple-pinched ray of merriment. She tucked the parchment into her dress. "Well, it's good to see you all the same."

Wesley nodded with a soft smile. "Same to you. We should be on our way."

Gwen stepped to follow him but stopped herself. "I almost forgot." She fished out twenty copper coins and placed them on the counter. "For the scones."

"Dear, this is too much," said Miss Shelley. "The scones only cost eight copper."

"I insist. Please, take it." Gwen shoved the pile further across the counter.

"Thank you greatly for your kindness."
"It was nice meeting you." Gwen waved at the two of them as she left the shop.

She returned with Wesley to the carriage, now void of barrels, and started their journey back to his estate. Tension filled the air that didn't exist before. They both had something on their minds, but neither one was willing to speak it. After a few leagues of riding, Gwen broke the silence.

"Those men back at the shop," she said, "they're members of the rebellion, aren't they? I noticed the red on their sleeves."

Wesley heaved an exasperated sigh as if answering the question lifted a weight from his chest. "Yeah. The rebellion occupied the town years ago. They took the local businesses hostage, forcing them to pay a protection tax, turned the tavern into a brothel, and took control of trade distribution to other cities. You can thank them for the increased cost of Sanduran wine throughout the continent."

"That shouldn't be possible," said Gwen. "As part of the truce, the rebels agreed to occupy a sanction of land near the estuaries. They shouldn't be anywhere east of the Blade's Trench."

"We thought so too. After a truce was made, we thought Perrotti and his band of stripes would leave the town, but that turned out to be wishful thinking."

"Stripes?"

"That's what we call them because... you know." He swiped a finger across his arm, referring to the red bands wrapped around their sleeves. "I'd do something about it, but Minks is a decent shot, and with Perrotti's other thugs, people would just end up getting hurt or killed."

"I wish I could help," said Gwen. She really did. If only there was a way for her to send word to her father that the rebels had violated the truce. He could send the soldiers to clear them out, but the Militia should already have been doing that. Instead, Sandur had been abandoned.

When they returned to the estate, Anden waited for them on the front porch. "Where have you two been?" he asked as Wesley halted the horses.

"Just went into town to take care of some business," said Wesley. "Took Gwen with me since she was starving and probably needed a good meal."

Not a word was spoken to Gwen, and none was needed. She felt his disapproving glare linger over her. He said to Wesley,

"When you get a chance, I'd like to discuss with you our issue."

"Fair enough," Wesley agreed. "We can talk over dinner. Got things I need to take care of around here while the sun's out."

For the rest of the day, everyone busied themselves with separate tasks. Gwen helped Wesley toil the vineyard while Anden inspected the chariot to see if he could get it running at normal speed again. Gwen paced up and down the rows of vines picking grapes. By the afternoon, she filled two buckets, which Wesley commended. As evening approached, they all regrouped inside, and Anden proceeded to tell Wesley about their situation and reveal Gwen's true identity as the princess.

10

Victoria never found the time to survey the palace gardens before. Usually, she was the one tardy for her private lessons. Tucked away in a secluded corner covered in lush, green vegetation, she waited. A mosaic of flora displayed their petals before her in an array of colors. Some were large, others small, and a few contorted into odd shapes. Unlike her sister, who frequented the gardens, Victoria couldn't name a single one, except maybe a rose. A gentle wind stirred them into a dance and carried any fallen petals into the foliage. She remembered a bouquet her sister gifted to her on one of her birthdays. It had long since withered and died, but she wished it hadn't. Upon her sister's return, Victoria would request another to be made and would care for it, not taking it for granted.

A nearby bush rustled as Kaylin Gunnway forced herself through. Her long, golden hair glowed in the sun, something Victoria envied. Her own golden locks draped over her head like noodles, the tips dipped in mud. She resented the tarnished color and kept it cut short, hovering just above her shoulders. Kaylin greeted her with a smile and warm embrace.

"Glad you're back," said Victoria.

"It would've been shorter if not for your father and the chancellor," Kaylin complained. "They insisted I rest until they were confident in my recovery. What kind of a captain am I if a little poke puts me out of commission like that?" She looked down at Victoria with sympathetic eyes. "How are you holding up?"

Victoria forced a smile. "Doing what I can. It's been hard not having you around. Father and Blackwood are a wreck."

"I've noticed," she said.

"Any word on Gwen?" Victoria asked, concerned.

"None, unfortunately." The Militia captain pried herself away from Victoria, dejected. No one understood her family's grief more. Being childhood friends, Kaylin was as much a sister to Gwen as she. Spinning around, her mentor wore a smile as radiant as her hair. "However, I have no doubt that we'll find her."

Victoria believed her. She had to.

Kaylin produced two sparring swords crafted from pliable wood and handed one to Victoria. "I hope you haven't been slacking off. Otherwise, you'll spend most of this session on your back."

Victoria snatched the wooden blade from Kaylin's grasp giving it a twirl. She reacquainted herself with its feel and weight as if the numbness in her arm had faded. Flourishing a few thrusts and strikes, she faced Kaylin with a smirk.

"You haven't lost your edge being hospitalized, have you?" she teased.

Kaylin removed her padded jacket. It tugged against her undershirt, allowing the scar on her side to peek out. The indent of tissue crawled from her hip nearly to the top of her stomach. Only a cruel piece of iron could leave such a wound. Taking her sword, Kaylin goaded Victoria to strike. Victoria charged, rearing her sword back. Kaylin's parry was almost lazy. She knocked the wooden blade aside and struck Victoria on the shoulder.

"Seems you have been slacking," Kaylin taunted. "You just lost your arm. Now, go again, and this time take it seriously."

Victoria steadied herself, pointing the blade with a single arm. Stepping forward, she feinted and aimed a strike at Kaylin's side, carrying the scar. The wood of their swords met, and they exchanged a series of blows. Her mentor checked each of Victoria's strikes staying on the defensive. It wasn't until a failed thrust that Kaylin adjusted her stance and switched to an offensive assault. Her strikes increased in speed as the wooden hilt twisted faster and faster in Victoria's grip. Their movements soon turned into a blur as her arm burned in an attempt to keep pace. With a single stroke, Kaylin knocked the sword from Victoria's grasp, tapping her with the blunt end on the cheek.

"That's more like it," said Kaylin. "With base swordsmanship, I'm sure you could beat a decent majority of my soldiers."

Victoria's eyes widened with excitement. "You think I could take the Exams?"

The Exams were various tests and trials that only those with the promise of being captains took. To pass meant one was qualified to hold such a rank and command an entire division of the Phoenix Militia. It was a badge of great pride and a signal of greater skill.

"Not yet," Kaylin responded bluntly. "You still rely solely on your physical strength. You've yet to tap into your greater potential." She tossed the sparring sword to the ground. "Speaking of which, it's time to practice meditation."

Victoria groaned in objection. For the first few years of training, she focused on getting into the best physical shape possible. The routine proved brutal as she performed various exercises and ran a minimum of three miles each day, but at least provided visible results. More recently, Kaylin added meditation after each sparring session to get in touch with her greater potential or some spiritual nonsense she never understood. It was part of the old traditions which allowed individuals to perform superhuman feats, but it was dying. Ever since the creation of REVs, implants boosting a person's capabilities through toxins, many abandoned the traditional ways for an easier alternative. Kaylin despised the implant's creation and forbade Victoria from getting one as a condition of her training. She also warned of REV overdose—an illness contracted from a high intake of toxins.

While she respected her mentor's wishes, Victoria couldn't deny the temptation she felt. All the time spent meditating and nothing to show for it. Kaylin assured that many soldiers struggled with achieving this awakening. It took her years to tap into this power and more to master it.

They lowered themselves onto the soft bed of grass and erected their backs into a proper sitting position. Victoria closed her eyes to help shut out the world around her and focus on nothing else but her own breathing. Barely a minute into meditation, a voice called out into the gardens.

"Captain Gunnway."

Kaylin sprang to her feet, pushing through the thicket of plants. Victoria followed her, curious to see who was calling. Exiting their personal sanctum, Ben Green wandered about looking for Kaylin.

"There you are," he said, making his way toward them. "Taking a stroll with the princess." He turned to Victoria with a stiff bow. "My lady." Something about his presence always set Victoria on edge. "I'm glad to see you've recovered," he said to Kaylin. "Would've been a shame if the supposed Militia's best was killed by a mere sellsword."

"What do you want, Green?" Kaylin snapped. Her glare was as sharp as one of her sabers.

"I'm here with Ambassador Krawczyk to report a sighting of Princess Guinevere in Lundur." His mouth curved into a slight grin at the shock plain on their faces. "Unfortunately, my men were unable to retrieve her. Some ruffian sped off in one of those self-propelled carriages."

"So, you lost her," chided Kaylin. Her interjection erased the grin from Green's face.

"My men lost her," he corrected. "And they're being reprimanded as we speak. If *I* were there, the princess would be here standing with us in the garden."

"She isn't, though." Kaylin stood nose to nose with Green, scowling. "And rather than searching yourself, you're currently parading around the palace like a prized lap dog."

Ben scowled right back at her. His hands clenched into fists hovering over the mace at his hip. "Let's not forget that it was during your absence that the heiress to the throne disappeared. As far as I'm concerned, the rest of us are cleaning up your mess."

Victoria wanted to lash out. Blaming Gwen's disappearance on Kaylin while she was gravely injured was more than insulting. It was vile. However, she bit her tongue. Even as a daughter to the king, there existed boundaries when dealing with a man like Ben.

Turning on his heels, he marched out of the gardens.

"Don't worry about mediating today," said Kaylin, heated. "Head back to your room and take a bath." She stomped off in the opposite direction leaving Victoria by herself.

Leaving the gardens, Victoria ventured up the endless staircase leading to her room. Reaching it, she prepared a bath, filling the tub with hot water. The muscles in her arm ached as she lowered herself in. Her face barely broke the surface as the rest of her body sank into the water. She stared aimlessly at the high, marble ceilings. A slight sense of relief washed away her fear but soon subsided. Her sister was alive and sighted in Lundur but taken somewhere else.

"Gwen," she whispered to the empty room. "Where are you?"

11

Wesley sat in an infinite silence, processing everything Anden had told him. Not a detail was spared, from their encounter in the capital to avoiding the Militia in Lundur and ending with their desperate escape from the fleshling horde the other night.

"That's heavy," said Wesley. "And that scene with the Militia is concerning. Gagging the heir to the crown and putting her in shackles. Just imagine what they'd do to the rest of us."

The breeze tickled the back of Gwen's neck through an open window as she leaned against the kitchen counter. "My father would never allow something like that. He tries to be a gentle man, but harming one of his daughters will turn him cruel in an instant."

"Something tells me your father would never have found out," chimed Anden. He sat across from Wesley at a table, drinking his flask as usual.

"If the rebels can occupy towns like Sandur," said Gwen, "do you think they would be able to infiltrate the Militia in some way?"

"I highly doubt it," said Anden. "Initiates start as children. They prefer it that way. No meaningful relations and ripe for indoctrinating them into service for the kingdom. To stage such a coup would take decades."

Wesley rose from his seat to light a few candles. "Could be the underground. The rebels may not convince them to turn sides, but enough money can tempt any man."

"What would the underground gain from kidnapping the princess?" challenged Anden. "They practically have the kingdom in their pocket already."

Wesley lit the last of the candles; their flickering light cast a soft glow. "This is all just one mess of a situation you've gotten yourself into."

Gwen lowered her head in shame as she crumpled a part of her dress in her hands. If she had never left the capital, none of this would have happened. "It's my fault," she muttered. "I shouldn't have left."

"I tried telling you that at the Muddy Mule." Anden took a swig from his flask.

"Tell me, my lady," said Wesley. "Why did you leave the capital, to begin with?"

"After my mother died, my father shut our family off from the world. He forbade both my sister and me to leave the palace unless it was under his orders. Growing up, all I ever knew was life within the palace, and as I got older, the pressure and expectation of taking the throne once my father passed weighed heavier on my shoulders. I turned to books, reading as much as I could about the continent, its history, divisions, cities, and cultures. I sought to understand the kingdom I would one day rule." Her arms trembled as her grip around the fabric of the dress tightened. She kept her head low, not looking at either Anden or Wesley.

"However, I came to the realization that no matter how many books I read, I may learn but never understand. I would never understand the various livelihoods of the vast array of people throughout the kingdom, the struggles and hardships they faced day to day. How could I rule over people and make decisions that affect their lives if I don't understand them?"

"I thought that's what the ambassadors were for," said Anden. "To help with that kind of stuff."

Gwen scoffed. "You don't honestly think all of them look out for the people they represent. I've met each ambassador, and some of them are only interested in themselves and their own power. I wanted to uphold the ideals of my father and be a ruler of the people."

"Sounds noble," chided Anden, "but still foolish."

Wesley grabbed an open bottle of wine on the counter near Gwen and poured himself a glass. "You could've waited until your coronation. All the power to go wherever you please."

"And have a veil thrown over my eyes touring cities as the queen?" said Gwen. "I wanted to see the continent for what it was. Raw with nothing hidden from me. Like the rebellion's occupation here in Sandur and the lack of protection to prevent it."

"I see your point," admitted Wesley, "but the world isn't a safe place for someone like you to be roaming on your own without some form of security. It would be best to return to the capital."

Gwen relaxed her hands and raised her head to see Wesley. His demeanor was calm but authoritative. He knew he was right, and so did she. It was hopeful thinking that she'd be able to make the journey across the continent without some form of retaliation. She would have to settle for the position thrust upon her.

The cry of a horse pierced the air, and the front door suddenly flew open as Miss Shelley raced inside.

"Wesley," she screamed. "Wesley, I need your help! Please!" Streaks of tears ran down her cheeks, her face contorted by despair. She buried it into Wesley's chest upon reaching him, sobbing and continuing to ramble incoherently.

Wesley grabbed her by the shoulders and pried her away from him. "What's wrong, Miss Shelley? What happened?"

"They took her," the shop owner said, half choking on tears. "I couldn't pay the debt, and they took her away." Wesley lowered her into a chair. Fetching some water, he handed her the glass and raised it to her lips to drink.

Anden scratched the patch of hair on his chin. "Who took who now?"

"Liz," Gwen breathed. "Her daughter, Liz. The rebels took her."

"Deep breaths, Miss Shelley," said Wesley, kneeling next to her. "I need you to calm down and tell me what happened."

Miss Shelley took a moment to compose herself, wiping the tears from her eyes. "When Minks entered the shop earlier today, he gave us a piece of parchment demanding we pay our debt in protection fees. When they returned to collect this evening, I told them I didn't have all the money. They said if I couldn't pay, then Liz would, and snatched her away. They took her to work in that forsaken whorehouse of a tavern and please any man that pays for it." She wrapped her arms around Wesley's neck in a somber embrace. "Please, help me. Help me get my daughter back."

"I'll see what I can do," he said, lovingly patting her on the back. "In the meantime, you should rest here for the night. It's too dangerous for you to ride home by yourself."

Wesley escorted Miss Shelley upstairs, disappearing for a considerable amount of time. Returning, he poured himself another glass of wine, which he knocked back before sitting in a chair. He rubbed his hands over his face, distraught.

"Sorry about all that," he said in a defeated tone.

Gwen stood from her chair and placed a comforting hand on his shoulder. He took hold of it, giving a gentle squeeze.

"How tough are their guys?" asked Anden.

"Not tougher than anything we've faced before," said Wesley. "Mostly just brawlers. Except for Minks. He has a sharp eye."

"Sharper than yours?"

"No, but enough to be a problem." He removed Gwen's hand from his shoulder. "This isn't a problem you need to concern yourself with. You've got enough to worry about already."

"You need help. That's all that matters," Anden said defiantly.

"Agreed," said Gwen. "The rebels shouldn't have been here in the first place."

Wesley wandered over to the window and stared at a lit candle. The tiny flame danced on the wick, fighting to stay lit against the wind. "We'll need a plan." He glanced over his shoulder at Gwen. "I don't want you risking your life, princess, but it could come to that."

Gwen swallowed her fear and provided an affirmative nod. "Whatever it takes."

12

Anden meandered through the dusty streets of Sandur on horseback. Gwen sat behind him, arms wrapped around his waist. The town was quiet as people minded their own business outside the various shops. Wesley trailed behind at a fair distance as they approached the stable. Dismounting, they handed the horse off to the stable hand and, with arms linked, headed toward the local tavern. Wesley gave a slight nod before sauntering further down the street in the direction of the pastry shop.

Pushing through the swinging doors, Anden and Gwen were greeted by the musky smell of ale and sex. Women adorned in thin veils of clothing strutted across the balcony above for the viewing pleasure of men below. He guided Gwen to the bar, where a barkeep in ragged clothes poured a glass of bourbon. As he returned the bottle to its place behind the bar, Anden got his attention.

"Excuse me, sir," he said. "The lady and I were looking for some pleasurable company to share."

The barkeep raised a curious brow. "Any request can be met with the proper amount of coin."

Anden slid a gold piece across the bar. "We'd like to see everything this establishment has to offer."

The barkeep's gaze lingered on the coin, then glossed over Anden and Gwen. Picking it up, he disappeared into a backroom for a few moments. Returning to the bar, he was followed by a man in a crimson pinstriped suit and bowler hat covering the dark curls of his hair. Two thin strips of a mustache twitched over his lips as he spoke.

"Good day to you, sir and madam," he said, shaking Anden's hand. "My name is Perrotti. Welcome to my establishment. Please, follow me, and I will show you our vast array of beautiful women."

He led them upstairs onto the balcony overlooking the rest of the tavern. A stocky man blocked their path upon reaching the stairwell. His eyes lingered on Gwen as they approached.

"My apologies," said Perrotti. "Rory here will first need to pat you down. Weapons are forbidden while enjoying our treasured delicacies."

His rough hands rifled through Anden's tunic and trousers. Unable to find anything, the thug turned to Gwen. He extended his hands, but she smacked them away.

"I didn't come to be fondled by some brute," she spat, shooting an icy glare at him.

He scowled at her, but Perrotti waved him off with a chuckle. "Leave the woman be. If the man is clean, that's good enough for me."

Rory stepped aside to let them pass. With a snap of Perrotti's finger, a line of twelve women in various colored dresses formed along the railing. Gesturing toward them, he said, "Take your pick of the litter. Anything that suits your fancy."

Anden looked to Gwen, who unlocked her arm from his and marched down the line, studying the face of each woman. Perrotti watched with a toothy grin as if he were presenting prized horses. Gwen moved down the line, stopping at about the seventh woman, and glanced back at the two men.

"This one will do fine," she said, pointing the finger at a slender, innocent-faced woman. She was petite in size, being a bit shorter than Gwen.

"Excellent choice," said Perrotti. He clapped his hands, and the rest of the women either returned to their rooms or continued strutting across the balcony. "Take all the time you need. Stay the night if you so choose." Striding back downstairs, Rory tugged on his arm to whisper something in his ear. He then returned to the backroom behind the bar.

Anden trailed behind Gwen as the woman guided them to their room. A quilted blanket covered the mattress at the center, most likely hiding any stains yet to be washed. Red curtains draped over the singular window, and a shabby armoire rested against the wall opposite of the bed. Anden closed the door behind them. The woman looked at Gwen with shock.

"Gwen," she said. "What are you doing here?"

"Your mother asked us to help you get out of this place," Gwen explained.

The woman averted her eyes to the floor and shook her head. "I can't. If I leave, they'll turn to torturing her and destroying her business. I have to do this to protect her."

"Wesley has offered his estate," said Anden. "You can both safely stay there."

"They'll find us," the woman muttered. "No matter where we hide, they'll find us."

Gwen gently touched her shoulder. "It'll be alright, Liz."

"In any case, we can cross that bridge when we get there." Anden signaled to Gwen, who removed her jacket. Reaching down the back of her dress, he pulled out the folded rods of his three-sectioned staff. Making his way to the door, he cracked it open. Gwen sat next to Liz on the bed as he peered through the sliver of an opening.

Between the gaps of the railing, Anden saw Wesley enter the lower floor. Approaching the bar, he traded a few words with the barkeep, who produced a tankard of ale. Downing a few gulps, he gestured toward a weasel-faced man with orange hair shouting, "Minks, we have a score to settle. Time to determine here and now who has the sharper eye. I challenge you to a game of daggers. Three throws each."

Minks smiled, accepting the challenge. The two men walked across to the far end of the room. On the opposite wall were three red rings and a black dot at the center. The length of their throws spanned across the entire tavern. Patrons gathered around as six daggers were laid out on two separate tables, three on each one.

"I'll be back once our path is clear," Anden said over his shoulder to the two women. With that, he crept through the doorway onto the balcony.

People gathered around Wesley and Minks, chanting as they rolled up their sleeves. Minks was the first to throw, picking up a dagger and flinging it at the wall. It stuck into the wood within the innermost circle, just shy of the center dot. Three wenches observed the contest leaning over the railing. He wrapped his arms around them.

"That seems to be quite the contest," he said with a charismatic grin. "We should go down and watch it up close. Drinks on me, of course." He flashed a few pieces of silver, sending the women into a fit of sensuous giggling. They strode across the balcony, and upon reaching the stairs, Rory shot him a glare. He handed the women the pieces of silver. "Go on ahead without me. I have some business to attend to first."

They continued down the stairs as Anden turned his attention to Rory, who stood as solid as a statue.

"The ladies wanted some time alone for the moment, but I want to make sure they're refreshed upon my return. Could you bring them some water to keep the fluids flowing, I'll say?"

"I'm not a butler," Rory growled. "You want water, get it yourself."

"Forgive me," said Anden. "I didn't mean to overstep my bounds. I'll fetch the ladies some water myself then."

Anden snatched his three-sectioned staff from behind his back and twisted one of the chains around Rory's neck. Squeezing with all his might, he kept the man from emitting a sound loud enough to penetrate the chants of the crowd. His arms flailed in an attempt to hit Anden as the chain wrapped tighter, turning his face red, then a shade of blue before his body grew limp. Anden dragged the corpse back to the room where Liz and Gwen still waited on the bed. Anden dropped his torso with a massive thud.

Anden turned to Liz, whose hands covered her mouth, looking at Rory's body. "Wesley said you'd know where the back door to this place is."

Closing her eyes, she took a few calming breaths. "It's behind the bar, past Perrotti's office."

"That means we'll have to go through the bartender."

Gwen smirked. "I can create an opening for you."

Anden glanced back through the door. Wesley threw his second dagger, piercing the rim of the center dot. Cheers erupted from the crowd. "It'll have to do," he said. "Wesley's distraction won't last much longer."

The three of them exited the room and headed downstairs to the bar. The barkeep stood idle as everyone was captivated by the contest. Gwen approached, fanning herself with her hand. "Pardon me," she said, "but would you be so kind as to fetch a lady some ale?"

"Ma'am." The barkeep grabbed a tankard and filled it to the brim with ale. Foam trickled down the side and onto the bar as he handed it to her. Picking up the drink, Gwen's grasp slipped, and the drink spilled over the floor behind the bar.

"Emperor be praised. I'm sorry about that."

The barkeep took a towel and, bending over, cleaned up the mess. Anden climbed over the bar, grabbed an empty glass and shattered it over the barkeep's head, causing him to collapse into the puddle of booze. Anden helped Liz and Gwen over the bar as well and entered the door in the back. They found themselves in a large warehouse stocked with barrels of wine, ale, and various other liquors. Some even stamped with the brandings of Bushgrove and Laminfell. The amount of supply would make any modest tavern owner envious. Eli would probably kill a man to have access to half the stock available here. They snuck through the room using barrels and stacked boxes as cover. Anden kept his eyes out for Perrotti or any more of his men, but not a soul could be spotted.

Reaching the end of the row of inventory, Anden whispered over his shoulder, "This looks like the right way, Liz?" There was no response. "Liz? Gwen?" A sharp click answered him. Anden turned around to see Perrotti and another thug pointing pistols at Gwen and Liz.

"Rory said you looked familiar," said Perrotti, pressing the barrel into Gwen's temple. "Recognized you yesterday in their shop. Seems Wesley convinced you into helping steal from me."

Gwen struggled to escape his grasp. "Liz is not your property."

"Oh, but she is. You see, her mother owed me a debt that she couldn't repay. In order to fulfill that payment, I took Liz here as an asset to my establishment, so in essence, she is my property." His beady eyes locked onto Anden. "It's a shame you decided to entangle yourself in this mess as well. Part of me really hoped you'd prove yourself to be a reliable customer." He motioned with the gun for Anden to give up his weapon and follow. "Come on, now. I have words I'd like to share with Wesley."

With pistols still aimed at the girls' heads, Anden fell in line between Perrotti and his henchman as they marched back out to the bar. People chanted as Wesley prepared to throw his final dagger, ending the contest.

"Sorry to interrupt," Perrotti roared. Everyone went silent, turning in shock to see the three of them captured. "But it seems Mr. Sparrow and his friends here developed this show as a scheme to steal from me. Minks, relinquish him of his weapon."

Minks pulled out his own pistol, aiming it at Wesley, who held up his hands in surrender. Reaching into the holster at Wesley's side, he removed the revolver and handed it to Perrotti.

"Now, seeing as I am an entertainer of sorts," Perrotti continued, "I too find this contest to be quite riveting. Although, I want to test your true marksmanship and see who really possesses the best shot in Sandur."

The barkeep stumbled to his feet from behind the bar, rubbing his head.

"Ah, Jorgy," Perrotti called out. "Perfect timing. Come over here and keep an eye on this one for me."

The barkeep hopped over the bar and took hold of Gwen as Perrotti snatched Liz from the other man's grasp, who then pointed his pistol at the back of Anden's head. The crimson-suit man guided Liz to the wall marked with the three rings. He pressed her back firmly against it and, taking a shot glass of bourbon from a patron, placed it on her head. She remained still as Perrotti paced over to Wesley, handing him the flintlock pistol.

OUT OF THE ASHES

"You each get one shot," he explained. "The one to knock the glass off her head wins. Don't worry if you kill her. I already have a replacement lined up," he said, sneering in Gwen's direction.

Locking the hammer back on the revolver, he pointed the barrel at Wesley. "Since I'm a generous man, you may have the first shot."

Wesley stared at the pistol in his hand, then at Liz. Their gaze held a thousand words, silent to everyone else. He raised his arm, taking aim. Her posture stiffened. His eyes never left hers as neither one of them trembled or flinched.

"Stop this," cried Gwen.

The barkeep clasped a hand over her mouth. "Shut it."

There was nothing they could do except watch the scene unfold. Wesley narrowed his eyes, taking a deep breath.

Bang!

A flash of smoke and Minks's dead body dropped to the floor with his head cracked open. Splatters of blood sprinkled members in the crowd, sending them into shrieks of terror. Perrotti pulled the trigger on the revolver, only to be met with a hollow click. He fired again and again, receiving the same result. Anden spun around, knocking the pistol out of the henchman's hand. It hit the floor, firing a round that startled the barkeep into releasing Gwen. She escaped into the crowd and forced her way to Liz's side. Anden unleashed a flurry of strikes into the henchman's abdomen, ending with a solid hook

111

to his jaw. It sent the man reeling onto a nearby table as the barkeep charged with raised fists.

Wesley ripped the revolver out of Perrotti's hand and delivered a solid punch to his face. A waterfall of blood spilled out of his nose, covering his thin mustache. Wesley buckled his leg and placed the revolver back into its holster.

"I've wanted to do this for a long time," he said, standing over the pitiful man cowering in fear.

The bartender was a decent fighter. He wasn't quick on his feet, but could certainly take blows. No matter how much Anden hit him, he kept swinging. Anden dodged and weaved through his strikes, connecting a jab every so often. They danced around the stampede of people rushing out of the tavern. It wasn't until the other henchman grappled him from behind that the barkeep connected a fist. His knuckles smashed into Anden's face, sending him into a daze. Another fist, this time to the chest.

"Wesley," Anden coughed. "A little help over here."

Wesley turned away from terrorizing Perrotti and hurried to offer aid. Catching the bartender's arm as he reared for another strike, Wesley swept his legs and twisted the man's arm until it snapped. Anden slammed the back of his head into the henchman's nose, breaking it. Slipping through his grasp, Anden grabbed a nearby chair and splintered it against the man's skull, knocking him unconscious. Everyone else cleared out of the tavern, leaving Anden and Wesley standing over two of Perrotti's men, Gwen and Liz hiding behind an overturned table, and Minks's corpse rotting on the floor. Perrotti was nowhere to be seen. Through the swinging doors, a red figure sprinted down the street. Pulling a man from his horse, he hopped onto the saddle and spurred it toward the horizon.

Wesley picked up the flintlock pistol next to Minks's body and sauntered out the doors, followed by Anden and the girls. Locking the hammer back, he raised his arm and stared down the sights of the barrel. Perrotti was a speck in the distance. Taking a deep breath, Wesley steadied his aim and pulled the trigger. The hammer clapped down in a plume of smoke as the gunshot echoed throughout the entire town. Perrotti's body remained on the horse for a moment before lifelessly falling off to the side.

Anden nodded approvingly. "Still got it."

Wesley tossed the pistol to the ground. "Always will." He approached Liz and caressed her cheek with his thumb. "You okay?"

"Yes," she said. "Thank you. Each of you." She glanced about at the three of them.

"Come on," said Wesley, "your mother will be glad to see you're alright."

Together, the four of them walked toward the pastry shop as people gathered in the streets murmuring about the madness they'd just witnessed.

The night was one of modest celebration. Wesley uncorked four bottles of what he considered to be the best wine he'd ever produced. They each took one and enjoyed it while expressing their merriment at Liz's safety and the liberation of Sandur. Gwen passed out with a quarter of her bottle remaining to which Anden took the liberty of finishing off. Liz was next, but to her credit, she had finished hers completely. After taking the women up to the beds, Anden and Wesley sat outside on the porch to finish the remainder of their drinks under the stars.

"Reminds me of the old days," said Wesley. "Fighting for our lives to share some booze at the end of the day."

"Risky move going in there with an unloaded pistol," said Anden, "but it paid off."

Wesley gave a casual shrug. "I figured you'd muck up the plan in some way."

"Fuck off."

The two shared a chuckle.

Anden fiddled with the bottle. "You know it'd really be like the old days if you left this vineyard behind and came with me."

Wesley pulled the drink from his lips. "Speaking of which, what's your next move?"

"Not sure," Anden replied. "Those soldiers back in Lundur, it made me think of the situation with Damian. Coincidence, or do you think I'm crazy?"

"Doesn't matter. You won't be able to run forever, not with her tagging along. You need to find some way to get her back to the capital. Otherwise, you both might end up dead."

Anden took a swig from his bottle. "I'm open to suggestions."

Wesley heaved a heavy sigh. "Talk it over with her in the morning. See if there isn't something you can come up with. I'll help in any way that I can 'cause I owe you one now."

"Just one?" Anden jested. "Don't think five years has made me forget about all the other times I've saved your ass."

"It has for me." Downing the rest of his wine, Wesley marched back into the house, patting Anden on the shoulder.

Anden gazed up into the night sky as he sipped the last of his wine. He couldn't deny the exhilaration coursing through his body after the day's events. It was a sensation he thought he had drowned long ago with empty years of drinking in taverns before settling in the capital's underbelly. While he had no intention of dying, an urge swelled within him, burning his chest. For the first time in a while, Anden felt genuinely happy.

13

Reed sought comfort in the calm sea breeze that rolled in with the tide. Amid the salty smell and starlit night, the lonely hillside washed away her concerns. The wind tossed her hair and caressed her face in a similar manner years ago when she was a young girl standing on the deck of a ship. She couldn't remember where in the continent it was. All her uncle told her was that she would see her mother. Five years it had been at that time since she last saw her mother, and despite it being the hour of the wolf, she waited. The ship rocked as the waves beat against the hull, causing it to creak. The deckhands ate and drank in the lower decks, but their laughter carried through the wood. All the while, she gazed out into the horizon.

She never saw her mother that night. Instead, a red glow burned in the distance, catching her eye as well as the rest of the crew's. Whispers circulated the deck of what it could be, but it wasn't until the following morning that the truth was revealed. Bandits raided a nearby town, killing or enslaving its inhabitants. Her uncle, along with her mother, were victims of the assault. The kingdom swept the event under the rug, never making any public statements. Only the word of distant spectators and twisted rumors were all that could be offered. Not even Elliot Durham knew the whole story other than they were told to never speak of it. She would often wonder if either of them survived.

A single tear fell down her cheek, and she was quick to dash it away. A leader may feel weak but never show it—a common phrase gifted unto her by her uncle. As a young girl, she learned to wear the mask of a leader. Around her generals and troops, she never let emotion get the better of her. It was during times like these, alone on the hillside, that the mask loosened.

"Taking a late-night stroll?" Elliot approached with muffled footsteps. If it weren't for his rusted voice, she wouldn't have noticed his arrival.

She did not turn to greet him. "I'm waiting to see if Watts returns." Her master engineer had been gone for days, testing his contraption.

Elliot joined her in overlooking the vastness of the sea. "I see. Things are certainly changing. People with carriages without horses, now that madman has somehow found a way to fly with the birds. I'm sure he'll be happy to hear what I'm about to share with you."

"Which is?"

"We've received word validating Vargo's claim. The eldest daughter to the king is indeed missing. They're keeping it a closely guarded secret, but more people are taking notice of the increased military activity. She was last seen in Lundur, but disappeared again." Dissatisfaction leaked into Elliot's words as he spoke. The fact that Vargo was able to procure such sensitive information no doubt troubled him. It definitely troubled her.

"It appears the information was worth the coin," she said. "Once Watts returns, I'll send out orders to begin preparations. With the weapon he's created, we'll bring the kingdom to its knees." Her emerald eyes glowed in the darkness of night as she faced her high overseer. "Any word from our eye on Vargo?"

"Nothing yet," responded Elliot.

"Regardless, he'll need to be summoned to help in our assault. He's a counter to the power of the Militia's captains."

"I understand," he said, "but I advise caution. A man able to come across such information so easily is dangerous in more ways than one."

"As I've said before, I don't trust Vargo." She brushed away strands of hair drifting into her face, so Elliot could clearly see the boldness it held as she spoke. "He's a tool. A useful one in accomplishing our goal. After that, we can discuss his disposal. In the meantime, be sure to keep our ears open for information regarding the princess. It benefits us if she stays missing."

"Of course." Elliot lifted his eyes to the stars as his rocky voice rippled the air. "I've noticed you've taken a liking to this particular spot these past few nights."

"If you have nothing more to discuss, then take your leave," Reed added a sharp edge to her words, unappreciative of Elliot's intrusion.

"Forgive me," he said. "I'm sure you're anxious for what is to come in the following days as we all are." He took his leave in silence, descending the hill.

Reed returned her attention to the endless void. The sea mirrored the stars in the sky so perfectly that it was difficult to tell where one ended and the other began. Reed was equally unsure of the outcome of this war lasting decades and surpassing a generation. Even with Watts' invention, taking the capital would prove arduous. Battles would follow in the wake of their victory as the other ambassadors would fight to retain any power left to them. Some may lay down their arms in surrender, but nothing was certain—almost nothing. One way or another, this was the start of the end. That much she knew.

A blinding light shined down on her from above. Shielding her eyes, Reed looked up to see the outline of Watts' creation blacking out the sky. With his return, preparations could now be made for the war's conclusion. Standing atop the hill and

silhouetted in the harsh light, she donned her mask once more.
A leader must never show weakness.

14

Gwen lay in bed, her head throbbing. It was the second time within the same week she drank so much to earn another hangover. Throwing the bedsheet over herself, Gwen closed her eyes in an attempt to sleep it off, but the sound of the door bursting open interrupted her. Gwen removed the sheet from her head to see Anden enter the room with an intense look.

"Come in, I guess," she grumbled, adjusting her pillow to cushion her back against the wall.

He sat down at the foot of her bed, looking pathetic but not in his typical drunken fashion. Something had beaten him sober and tossed him at her doorstep. "How do you plan on returning to the capital?" he asked. "As courteous as Wesley is, you can't stay here forever. The Militia will come eventually."

Gwen hadn't really thought about it. She hugged her legs to her chest. "I don't know. It's not as simple as jumping on a horse and riding east. Unless I want to risk having another run-in with those creatures."

"It seems you're not completely airheaded," Anden teased. "If you're wanting to go anywhere, you'll need an escort."

She narrowed her eyes. "You? You said you couldn't go near the capital, not in this climate. Perhaps Wesley can—"

"Wesley will only offer the same response I have."

Her heart sank. "He's a criminal?"

"You'll find there's a lot of us throughout the continent," Anden stated.

"I'll find a hunter then," she said with confidence. She could tell Anden was playing some sort of game with her. "One could take me back to the capital without issue."

"True," he said, "but say you come across a group of soldiers like the ones in Lundur who chain you up with a gag in your mouth. I wouldn't be too hopeful for the hunter to step in. They aren't meant to interfere with the kingdom's affairs and won't start a fight with the Militia."

He was making a point, baiting her. "What will it cost then?"

"Thirty silver. A discounted rate since I can't take you straight to the capital."

Gwen's face scrunched into a look of irritation. "I'll consider myself blessed. So, do you have any ideas on getting me back to capital without taking me there?"

He pursed his lips and scratched the hair on his chin. "You said you met each of the ambassadors. Staking your life on it, are there any you trust?"

She contemplated the thought. Out of all the ambassadors outside the capital, there was one she trusted completely. One she'd known from adolescence and spent hours combing through books with in the palace library. "Ambassador Archer. She can be trusted."

Serving as an attendant to Ambassador Yensin, Noreen Archer often frequented the palace where Gwen was able to see her. Being around the same age, the two developed a lasting bond, and Noreen promised when Gwen took the throne, she would become chancellor, and together, they would stabilize the kingdom. Her intellect and dedication caused Noreen to soar in the political sphere as she was chosen to be Yensin's replacement, governing the Third Division and becoming the youngest ambassador ever elected at twenty-one years.

Anden unleashed a guttural laugh, one that shook his slender frame. It was off-putting to witness after only seeing him chuckle when it was to mock her in some way. "Noreen Archer, the ambassador stationed at Danforth, the Militia's headquarters? Out of all the choices, you sure know how to pick them." He rose from the bed with a smirk tugging at his cheek. "I'll get you to Danforth, but we'll need the help of another criminal. The only one to ever sneak out of such a fortress."

Gwen tossed her legs over the side of the bed, sitting anxiously. "Who?"

"His real name is Damian," said Anden, "but you're probably familiar with his nickname, the Burnt Coat."

Fear gripped Gwen's heart. The legend of the Burnt Coat was infamous. The tale of a Militia captain who slaughtered his own men wove its way into every soldier's memory. No one knew why he betrayed his men, but many claimed he was a raving lunatic. She would hear those standing guard at her bedroom door murmur the story to each other. Branded a traitor, the executioner came for his head; however, he avoided such a fate. The details regarding his escape differed each time the story was told. Some claimed he dug a hole out of his cell, while others said he'd fought through hordes of soldiers, and few believed the Hand of Death had set him free. Despite their differences, every version ended the same way. He vanished. A ghost of the Militia's past they wished to forget.

"You can't be serious," said Gwen, shooting off the bed. "The Burnt Coat is a vile monster."

"Hold your tongue before talking about things you know nothing about." His copper eyes pierced her soul as anger seethed in his voice. It was so sudden that it shook Gwen to her core. "If you don't want my help, fine, but if you do, be ready to leave by the afternoon. I'll see if Wesley can offer us any supplies for our journey."

He marched out of the room, slamming the door shut. Gwen was unsure how to feel about the situation. She'd never seen Anden get aggressively defensive, all because she called a known traitor to the kingdom vile. Questions swirled in her head, causing it to throb more. How will they find a man who disappeared off the face of the earth? How can they be certain he'd actually help them? Who exactly was the man she happened to meet back in the capital?

As the morning waned, the sunlight saturated the leaves and wrappings of the vines in the vineyard. Surrounded by the greenery, Gwen daydreamed of her daily strolls through the palace gardens. She loved marveling at the array of flowers ranging from roses to orchids and even flame lilies. As a little girl, she would even talk to them as if they were close friends. They never talked back, only listening, and at times, that's all she needed. If only she could return to an age of such innocence, spared from the burden of responsibility. Overlooking the estate, the perspective of Wesley's house was familiar in a way. It mirrored the painting on the wall she saw the morning after their arrival. She pictured the two blobs as Wesley's parents toiling the land.

The wind carried a voice, beckoning to her. "Lady Gwen."

Gwen awoke from her daydream to see Liz shouting her name as she hurried over. Her joyous smile had not left her face since the previous night. It was an enigma how her cheeks had not grown sore.

"Lady Gwen," she repeated, "Anden said he's ready to depart and asked for me to come fetch for you."

Gwen followed her to the front of the house, where Wesley placed some provisions in the back compartment of the chariot. She gave him a curtsy upon her advance. "Thank you for letting us stay here," she said. "May the winds bring good tidings." Wesley responded with a smile and a nod. After hugging Liz, Gwen climbed into the seat next to Anden.

"What's your heading?" asked Wesley, resting an arm on one of the doors.

"Nabal," said Anden. "Word among the hunters throughout the years is Damian sought refuge with the Core. If that holds true, a bookkeeper should know his location."

"Bookkeeper?" Gwen had heard many stories about the Core but never anything of a bookkeeper.

"Whenever a hunter completes a contract, they send a report to an outpost," Anden explained. "Helps tally a hunter's reputation as well as track the amount of creature activity throughout the continent. The ones who keep those records are the bookkeepers, and there are several in Nabal."

"Sounds like a plan," said Wesley. "Good to know I'm not throwing myself into utter chaos." The chariot lurched sideways as he vaulted into the backseat.

"What are you doing?" Anden asked, taken aback.

"Figured I'd come along," Wesley answered, melting into the seat with no intention of moving. "I thought about what you said last night, and that skirmish did get me feeling a bit nostalgic."

Wesley's charisma infected Anden, stretching a smile across his face.

Gwen whipped around, flabbergasted. "What about the vineyard?"

"Liz can take care of it for me. She's more than capable." He shot her a wink turning her cheeks rosy.

"There's no guarantee you'll make it back," said Anden.

"Good." Wesley kicked his feet up, placing his hands behind his head. "I'd be disappointed if there were."

With a twist of the key and pulling some levers, the chariot roared to life, spitting out its plumes of black smoke. Pushing a pedal, they veered off down the dirt pathway away from the estate. Wesley looked over his shoulder, holding an eternal gaze with Liz as she waved them goodbye. He didn't tear his face away from the horizon until she faded from sight.

15

The king rested on the bottom step of the staircase leading up to the throne with a glazed look in his eyes. Since his daughter's disappearance, he did little else than sulk in isolation. Blackwood's resonant footsteps broke the somber stillness encompassing the room. He squatted down next to Peter.

The king forced strength into his voice. "Has there been any word on Gwen?"

"Not since the incident in Lundur," Blackwood replied. "The men reported her kidnapper rode in a machine-powered carriage. Most likely a noble or someone of wealth."

The king hung his head. With each passing day, he grew weaker from his daughter's absence. The longer she remained missing, the sooner they would have to face the fact that she may never return. It saddened Blackwood to see his friend, the man he admired, crumble at the base of his throne.

"We've been questioning anyone suspected to be in the northern wing of the palace during the fire and sellsword attack. Nothing truly insightful has yet been presented."

The hinges of Peter's metal brace squeaked as he staggered up the stairway. "Hopefully, something will arise. The culprit who tried to kill me could've also taken my daughter."

Blackwood watched the old king ascend the throne. The faint glow of the pale moonlight kissed his silver hair white. Reaching the top, he eased himself into its ivory clutches.

"Is there something else you wished to discuss?" he asked.

Blackwood climbed the stairs as well, unveiling a piece of parchment. "Word from Lawson in Papuri. Reports of people seeing strange lights off the coastline in the archipelago. They described it as fire raining from the sky." He handed the parchment to Peter.

The king skimmed the scrawled letters staining the page. "Probably a volcano erupting on one of the distant islands. Nothing more."

Blackwood bowed deeply, respecting the king's word. With nothing else to discuss, he bid Peter farewell. "Try to get some rest. Hopefully, in the coming days, promising developments will arise."

The king muttered under his breath a series of strange noises and sounds foreign to Blackwood's ears. "*Fûh ries wûren delenr ihrae teiaerna.*" He delivered the words with a heavy voice. "One of the few phrases we've deciphered from the ancient texts. It's a wishful expression, 'may the winds bring good tidings.' By the saints, we need that more than ever."

Blackwood couldn't agree more.

He left the king sitting on the throne and exited the room. Wandering the halls, he bumped into Mary Katherine. Her body tensed in alarm as she recoiled away before realizing it was him. The light she emitted in his office not so long ago faded, showing her age.

"How is the king?" she asked.

"Not good," said Blackwood. "The sooner we can find Gwen, the better."

"I hope so." Her voice was a whimper. "It's already been a few days since her last sighting."

Blackwood wrapped his arms around her in a comforting embrace. "We'll find her," he assured. He held her in his arms, hoping time would slow for an eternity. With each day spawning more problems, sharing tender moments such as these was scarce. She placed gentle hands on his cheeks and tilted his head down for a kiss. Usually, they avoided displaying their affection in the open for anyone to see, but they needed this. Their lips parted, and she pressed her forehead against his.

"I await the day we can put the issues of the realm aside," she whispered, "and only worry about us."

"Me too," he said. After holding each other for a few brief moments, they pulled away. Blackwood stared at her with his dark eyes. "Until then, we still have a duty to uphold."

"Which reminds me," she said, adjusting her hair, "I have a list of a few nobles stated being present in the northern wing at the time of the attack. I've issued them all a summons for questioning, but they've refused, claiming to be too busy."

"Leave it to highborn nobles to make everything more difficult," sighed Blackwood. "I'll pay them a visit personally. Hard to refuse questioning when the chancellor shows up at your door. Is that all?"

Mary Katherine remained in front of him, coy. "Will you share my bed with me tonight?"

Blackwood hesitated to answer. He wanted to but was unsure if such action was wise. Any time they slept together, it was at an inn, shrouded in disguise so as not to cause scandal. Within the walls of the palace, someone might notice and expose their relationship. Blackwood didn't want that for her, as the other members of Parliament would use it as a weapon to gut her and despise him even more. He should refuse but he couldn't. He yearned for her, and love turned wise men foolish. "Fine," he whispered, "just for tonight."

16

Blackwood left Mary Katherine's chamber at the break of dawn so as not to be seen by anyone. Entering his chamber, he locked the latch of the door and rested on a cushioned stool. He could still feel the weight of Mary Katherine's body against his. The nights of Vargo tormenting his dreams diminished into memories in her presence. It was his first full night of sleep since the day of the truce.

He disrobed from his night tunic and prepared a bath. After cleaning the stench of yesterday's sweat, he donned his formal attire, slicked back his hair, and groomed his beard. Studying his reflection in the mirror, he scanned down, then up, then back down again. Everything fit together to form the regal appearance the Chancellor of Parliament should have. Satisfied, Blackwood left his chambers to fetch some breakfast. A long day of squabbling with nobles awaited him, and he wanted to get as early a start as possible. Servants and soldiers now wandered the halls in droves as the sun drifted over the sea. In the Great Hall, Helmond, the royal cook, served him eggs, potatoes, and two chewy strips of bacon. Blackwood was quick to eat, careful not to stain his immaculate, white clothing. Mary Katherine entered at the tail end of his meal. She didn't sit with him and instead placed herself at a table opposite of his. Glancing up, he noticed her shoot a soft smile in his direction. She held no grudge for his morning absence, aware of the reputation they needed to maintain. With his meal finished, he marched out of the Great Hall and called on two Militia soldiers to bring a carriage and escort him out of the palace.

They procured him the palace's only self-propelled chariot. Its mighty roar startled Blackwood upon its approach. The polished steel reflected his image like a mirror it was so clean. Blackwood was amazed with the creations master engineers were producing and wondered what ends they would achieve in the future. Climbing into the back seat, they departed into the city.

They traveled a northern road where many aristocrats resided. The noble houses were unique in structure, presenting towering pillars and domed brass rooftops. The windows were arched, sometimes stretching half the height of the building. Some were so large and elaborate they could almost overshadow Ser Titus' Basilica. During his ride, Blackwood studied the list Mary Katherine had given him. Ten names in all.

The first on the list was Berthold Farlow, a charismatic elder who took people's opinions of him to heart. He was shocked to find the chancellor knocking on his door but offered a gracious welcome. It took a while for Blackwood to get the information he needed as the ornery man preferred to take wide tangents detailing his odd hobby of keeping bees. He even offered Blackwood the opportunity to see the hives he kept. The chancellor declined, stating he had other business to attend.

The others were not so talkative. If it hadn't been for his status as chancellor, half of them would have slammed the door in his face. Nobles tended to have high opinions, setting themselves on a level nearly equal to the king. One after the other, Blackwood questioned about the day of the truce getting similar responses. None of them possessed an inkling of an idea nor provided any evidence of how the sellswords infiltrated the palace. It was well past midday by the time he reached the last name on the list, and all Blackwood had to show for his efforts was weariness.

The chariot halted at their final stop. It was a singular tower spanning several floors crowned with a wide dome. The two soldiers flanked Blackwood as he provided three solid knocks to the front door. Thomas Walsh, a man with butterscotch hair, curled mustache, and pointed goatee, answered. He had flawless skin, wore a silk, purple tunic, and each of his fingers was decorated with a gemmed ring.

"Chancellor Blackwood," he said, giving a small bow. "I was not expecting you."

"I was not to be expected," Blackwood replied. "May I come in?"

"Of course." Walsh bid him welcome with a wave of his hand.

Blackwood motioned for his men to remain outside. The interior was decorated as lavishly as the man's fingers. Antiques and artifacts plated with silvers and gold filled the room. A glass shelf brimming with chalices of all makes and sizes dominated the far corner. It was evident the man had an interest in collections.

"To what do I owe the pleasure of your presence?" he asked. The locks of his hair draped over his angular face, hiding his high cheekbones.

"Since you have had trouble finding time to honor a summons at the palace, I've decided to pay you a visit myself regarding questions on the day of the truce."

He forced a smile. "Ah, yes. I have been very busy these past few days. Even now, you interrupt my work."

"You are not the only one," said Blackwood in a rueful tone.

"Continue your work as we talk, then. It's just a few questions, nothing too distracting."

"Very well."

Blackwood followed him up a spiraling staircase to his study on the third floor. The nobleman perched himself at his desk with a wall-sized bookcase serving as the backdrop. He prepared a piece of parchment, dipping a quill in a vial of ink, and began scribbling. Paintings lined the other walls, and Blackwood glanced about at each of them. One depicted the images of Edward's Sanction of Saints who helped him stand against his brother, Harrod the Tyrant, and the vassal lords that ruled over the kingdom. There were seven in total seated at a round table. It reminded him of the Tomb when the ambassadors would all gather at a conclave to discuss the realm's issues. Another was a portrait of King Edward, most likely a replica of the one found in the palace. The third one caught his attention. A fleet of ships battled amid a raging storm. Lightning erupted from the dark clouds, and the waves rammed into the hulls of the ships, splashing onto the decks.

"Brilliant piece," Walsh commented, catching Blackwood staring. "A depiction of the bout in the Battle of Brothers. The place where the tyrant, Harrod, suffered defeat against his younger brother. It's inspiring, hence why I have it my study."

"Where did you get it?" asked Blackwood.

"Some old geezer off the coast of Papuri had it as a family heirloom. Apparently, it was painted by one of his forefathers who witnessed the battle. Looking at it, you would believe him. It feels like you're actually there. Took a fair amount of coin to convince him to part with it."

"A fan of history," said Blackwood. "Especially of the Battle of Brothers and the era of King Edward."

Walsh continued scribbling on the parchment. "It's good to know one's history, or they might be doomed to repeat it. The kingdom should've taken heed of that. Some could say the Red Rebellion is the second coming of Edward's rebellion. Lucius certainly followed in the footsteps of his tyrannical ancestor." With a sharp flick of his wrist, he marked his signature at the bottom of the page. "Not to be rude, Chancellor, but if you wouldn't mind asking your questions. I could talk about history all day, but I'm sure we're both short on time for that."

"Too true," agreed Blackwood. He paced toward the other end of the study, where it extended out to a balcony. "We have statements placing you in the northern wing of the palace where the sellswords started the fire."

"The fire. I coughed up smoke for two days after that little scare."

The sea sparkled in the sunlight from the view of the balcony. To Blackwood's right loomed the royal palace over the cliffside. "Did you perhaps notice anything strange of anyone or how the sellswords might have gotten in?"

Walsh heated a stick of wax over the flame of a candle. "For an instant, I saw those ruffians tip over a few candelabras setting the curtains ablaze before I turned tail and ran off. Other than that, I'm afraid I don't have much to offer."

At the edge of the balcony, Blackwood noticed a telescope resting on the railing. "And you have no idea how they might have infiltrated the palace?" Peering into the eyepiece, the vast, blue sky filled his vision.

"None," said the nobleman. "I was just as shocked as everyone else upon seeing them."

Blackwood adjusted the telescope, aiming it toward the cliffside just beneath the palace. Focusing the blurred image, he found the ledge he once stood on with Rahm and Captain Green and there carved into the cliff was the entrance to the mines.

"Something catching your eye?" asked Walsh. He stood at the threshold of the study with a sealed parchment in his hand.

Blackwood pulled away from the telescope, adjusting it back to its original position. "Just admiring. Never really used such a tool before. Share a similar curiosity with astronomy as history?"

He smirked. "A close second. Do you have any more questions for me?"

"If that's all the information you can offer, I have no reason to linger." Blackwood mirrored his smirk. The nobleman guided him back down to the main floor. Bidding him farewell, Blackwood strode back to the chariot with his soldiers. He whispered to one of them, "Until ordered otherwise, I want every parchment both delivered and sent from that man's estate brought to me." Blackwood may have solved the mystery behind the mine entrance's discovery, but he needed hard evidence of Walsh's betrayal before making him sing.

17

The northern forests were a pleasant change of scenery from the flat, open lands they previously traversed. Gwen preferred the leaves' lively colors dancing in the breeze above to the muted brown and orange tones of the countryside. Splashes of light penetrated the foliage from endless rows of trees stretching into the heavens. Anden maneuvered the carriage slowly along the trail. Every now and then, a large root jostled them around as the terrain was meant more for a horse than a mechanical behemoth plowing over everything. Wesley sat up front next to Anden sharing ample conversation while Gwen sprawled across the back seat enjoying the ride.

"We're getting close," said Anden.

They followed a faint whisp of smoke snaking through the trees and reached an encampment hidden in the wilderness. Anden halted the carriage in front of a wall crafted from tree trunks with ends carved into spikes. Two hunters clothed in animal hides stood guard at the gate, glaring at them.

"What business do outsiders like you have here?" one of them asked. The tangles of his beard were lost in the furs of his coat.

"We've come looking to recruit a hunter," explained Anden.

"Unusual for commoners to journey here just looking to hire a hunter's blade."

"It's a pretty unusual job." He took out a small pouch jingling with coin and tossed it to one of the guards. "Want to make sure we hire the right guy."

The hunter caught the pouch, checking it, before looking to the other. "Leave that contraption outside the gate. Don't need it getting in anybody's way."

The gate cranked open as they exited the chariot. Members of the Hunters' Core were a people of the land. Everything within the encampment was constructed utilizing materials available throughout the forest. Tents crowded the ground and, in the canopies above, a series of ladders and bridges connected a village of cottages. The structures were an extension of the forest seemingly built by nature rather than man. It was a wonder to behold, unlike anything described in Gwen's books. Hunters tended to their business, paying them no mind as they entered. One of them flaunted a belt of skulls as he paraded through the camp. Others simply carried scars on their skin but were just as battle-hardened and forged by the anvil of combat.

"Any idea where the bookkeepers might be?" asked Wesley glancing about the camp.

"None whatsoever," replied Anden. "Could try asking around for some information. Hunters aren't a sociable lot, but there might be a few loose-lipped ones at whatever watering hole they serve alcohol at."

Gwen raced around Anden, blocking his path. "We're here to find the bookkeepers, not share drinks."

A frown soured his face. "Listen, princess. I don't need your royal permission to get a drink." He took a step forward to pass her, but Gwen shifted over, cutting him off. She crossed her arms, glowering. It was his idea to search for the Burnt Coat, despite her opposition, so that's precisely what she expected from him. Not leisurely strolling into taverns for drinks. "Fine," he said, defeated. "Then how do you suggest we find a bookkeeper? Keeping in mind you didn't know what one was before we left Sandur."

Gwen bit her lower lip. As much as it frustrated her, Anden had a point, but she stood her ground, trying to think of something.

"Gwen?" a voice called out. Amid the crowd of hunters, a familiar head of matted, greasy hair stepped through.

"Johnny," Gwen said, baffled. She shouldn't be surprised seeing him at a Core outpost, but it was a coincidence nonetheless. "Fancy seeing you here."

"I should be saying that to you." He studied Anden and Wesley, standing behind her in an uneasy silence.

"Oh," she chirped, breaking the ice, "these are hired hands of mine. Helping me in my travels. Anden and Wesley."

Wesley extended a hand toward the hunter, but Johnny ignored it. His gaze lingered on the revolvers strapped to Wesley's hips. "At least you got yourself some protection."

Anden stepped forward, angling his nose high in the air. "If you don't mind me asking, where did you meet our lovely Gwen here?"

"She stumbled into my camp looking for warmth in Lundur. Needing a place to stay, I escorted her to The Seaside Cottage." Anden muttered something under his breath, but Johnny didn't seem to hear. "I heard the Militia raided the inn. Stirred up so much chaos, I decided to head back to headquarters. It's good to see you're unharmed." He flashed a smile to Gwen before turning his hardened face back to Anden. "So, what brings you to the outpost?"

Anden answered guardedly, "Looking to gain an audience with a bookkeeper. Need to know the last location of a specific hunter."

Johnny rubbed a hand over his stubbled jaw. "The bookkeepers here are quite busy, not sure they have time to deal with commoners."

Anden breathed heavily, pinching the bridge of his nose. Digging through his trousers, he fished out five silver pieces and placed them in Johnny's hand. "Perhaps they'd be more willing to meet a friendly face."

Gwen watched as the hunter pocketed the coin. Throughout the exchange, she noticed Wesley subtly kept a hand near one of his pistols.

"I'm sure they will," said Johnny. "So, what's the name of the hunter you'd be looking for?"

"Damian Briggs."

Johnny's sunken eyes grew dark. Gwen could feel a shift in the atmosphere. "An interesting man to be looking for."

"Hence why I included a bit extra," said Anden.

The hunter tilted his head, looking Anden over once more. "Fair enough. Shall I meet you here after acquiring the information?"

"Actually, if you wouldn't mind pointing me the in the direction of a tavern or something similar, I would like to have a drink while I wait."

Johnny directed him toward the mess hall, a hut crafted entirely from branches. Anden set off before Gwen could object, leaving her to thin her lips in contempt.

The hunter turned to her and Wesley. "And you two?"

144

Gwen had no interest in sitting in a bar. Between the Muddy Mule, Seaside Cottage, and the tavern in Sandur, she gathered them not to be places for her enjoyment. "I'd prefer to take a walk around the forest. Not sure if I'll ever be able to see it again after this."

Johnny pointed a finger beyond the other end of the camp. "There's a field not too far from here. Good for sightseeing. I'll grab your friend and meet you there."

Gwen nodded, and they parted ways. Wesley joined her as she crossed the gate into the dense forest. They followed a narrow path of dead leaves that crumbled with every step. The echo of their crunches grew more prominent the further they traveled, and less light penetrated the weave of branches above. Darkness crept in as Gwen felt a presence looming over them. She shook the feeling by striking up a conversation.

"Wesley," she said, "how long have you known Anden for?"

He ran a hand through his beard, combing it. "We go way back. Worked a gig together serving a noble. Spent most of our time escorting him around the continent while he did business."

"So, how did you end up becoming wanted criminals?"

He searched the ground for an answer as if it were hidden in the leaves. "That's a matter we promised not to talk about. For our own safety."

Gwen didn't know what else to expect. He didn't seem to be a bad man, but whatever crime he committed must have stained his reputation greatly to take an oath of silence regarding the matter. If he and Anden were criminals, as they said, why would they help her?

Continuing along the path, they reached an opening in the foliage. Stepping out of the shade, they stood before a gaping field where the grass stretched high, covering Gwen's lower body. A gust of wind sent the blades into a wild dance like waves of a mighty, green ocean.

Wesley shielded his eyes from the sun. "Having spent so much time in the country, I've forgotten how beautiful the rest of the continent can be."

Gwen grazed a hand through the grass, their tips tickling her palm. After traversing the dark forest, being under the open sky felt tranquil. She twirled around, making the blades of grass bow as she processed through. This was what she longed for when leaving the palace, the serenity and pureness offered by the land. Witnessing the wonders described in the books she constantly read. She was content. Still, the moment was short-lived as Wesley tackled her to the ground. The tall grass engulfed them as she heard the faint whistle of an arrow piercing the air. Wesley's eyes were tiny, yellow beads staring at her in panic.

"Stay low," he whispered. Pulling himself off her, he rose from the vegetation, hands resting on his pistols, ready to draw in an instant.

Gwen peered through the thicket of grass to see a figure, cloaked in black, drift through the field from the edge of the forest. The veil of the dark hood concealed their identity. Wesley clutched the grip of his pistols.

"Who are you?" His booming voice shook the air. The figure advanced unintimidated, only stopping after Wesley drew one of his pistols. "Answer me."

The figure brandished a peculiar-looking bow in the shape of a ribcage, sprouting limbs that were tied together by a string. From its other sleeve, it produced an arrow, off-white in color and sharpened like a fleshling tooth.

"Hand over the girl."

Wesley narrowed his gaze. "Not happening."

He fired a shot. An arrow careened out of the air and into the grass. Gwen shook herself as if to confirm what she witnessed was not a figment of her imagination. Wesley managed to shoot the arrow off its trajectory, but the concerning part was Gwen didn't see the figure draw its bow.

A malicious sneer crept across its thin lips. It spoke with a shrill and tart voice, "Seems killing you may not be as boring as I thought."

The bloodlust emanating from its presence drowned Gwen. The pressure pressed against her chest, making it difficult to breathe. Not even the soulless gaze of the fleshling that marked her filled her with such fear. Wesley appeared to be equally shaken as a bead of sweat pierced his brow. He pulled back the hammer for another shot but suddenly jerked his head to the right. A gash cut across his left cheek, seeping blood.

"Sharp reflexes," the figure jested. "Let's see how long you can last."

Wesley drew his other pistol, and the crack of the gunshot sent Gwen cowering into the thicket. She pressed her hands against her ears as more gunfire erupted over her. She could feel the blades shift as Wesley moved, staying close to where she lay. She wasn't sure how long the skirmish lasted. Only when the shots ceased did she uncover her ears and look up to see Wesley standing over her bloodied. His body was covered in cuts, and smoke drifted off the barrels of his pistols. Heavy breaths poured from his chest as he remained still.

"Out of rounds?" said the figure. "Such a shame. You were quite the plaything, but I think it's time to put you down."

It readied one final arrow, pinching it against the bowstring. Wesley closed his eyes, accepting his fate as the cloaked figure drew its bow. Gwen shot up from the grass and extended her arms out wide, shielding Wesley.

The figure lowered its weapon. "Look at this. Seems the princess has some guts after all."

"Gwen, get out of here," said Wesley, wincing in pain.

Gwen didn't run. She glanced over her shoulder at the man painted red in his own blood. "I don't want to see you die like this. It's only trying to kill you because it wants me."

"Don't flatter yourself, honey," the figure said. "I was going to kill him whether you came willingly or not." It drew its bow once more, but the arrow flew past Gwen and Wesley upon firing, knocking a hatchet to the ground.

Johnny raced up beside them, wielding a sword with Anden clutching his signature three-section staff. Wesley shoved Gwen behind him with both pistols raised. The minor distraction gave him enough time to reload. The three men stood against the mysterious figure.

"Damn," it said in disappointment. "I was told not to garner too much attention. Seems capturing you won't be as easy as originally thought." Its thin lips curled into a chilling smile as a gust of wind ripped through the field, tossing a torrent of leaves and grass into a spiral. As the wind died down and the leaves fell, the figure disappeared.

Wesley holstered his pistols, barely able to stand. "Good thing you came when you did."

"What the hell was that thing?" asked Anden.

"We should head back to the camp," said Johnny picking up his hatchet. "That thing could still be lingering about."

Gwen and Anden assisted Wesley back to the encampment. The blood leaking from his wounds darkened the blue jacket wrapped over her shoulders. Even with a seasoned hunter like

Johnny escorting them, Gwen glanced around, afraid that whatever attacked them could still be lurking in the shadows. Its dark aura left an imprint clutching her chest. She considered them lucky to have survived. Entering the camp, Johnny sought medical attention for Wesley. His body was cleansed of blood and wrapped in a layer of bandages. After his wounds were tended to, Johnny proceeded to relay the information gathered from the bookkeeper.

He crossed his arms as a somber expression stretched down his face. "Not sure if the news I'm about to give you is good or bad after what just happened." Gwen could see his nails digging into the skin of his arms as he forced the words out. "Damian's last recorded job was down in Kelveux."

Gwen recognized the name. Kelveux was considered a cursed town given its proximity to the Demons' Cavity. Overrun with horrid creatures, the only living souls occupying it were hunters. It was the only place she hoped to avoid in her travels, but given her luck so far, it fit right into their journey.

"Great," sighed Anden. "Should've figured we'd be going to that ghost town."

"I'd rather deal with those beasts than that thing in the cloak," said Wesley. With his shirt and leather vest back on, only the bandages on her arms were visible.

"We should hit the road," said Anden. "It's a long trip, and there's no guarantee Damian will still be there." He headed toward the gate with Wesley on his heels.

Gwen moved to follow as well, but Johnny pulled her aside. Unstrapping the sheathed short sword at his hip, he handed it to her. "Take this. Looks like you might need something to protect yourself. Guess I understand a bit more why you're looking for a man like Damian." He clasped his hand on hers as she reached to take the sword. While worn with calluses, it was soft to the touch. Hard to imagine hands like these were used to kill. "Take care of yourself, Gwen. It seems more and more monsters crawl out of the dark corners of the continent."

"Thank you," she said. Pecking his cheek with a kiss, she took the sword into her grasp. It was heavier than expected. She might be able to swing it around a few times, but it was better than nothing. It pulled at her hip as she strapped the blade around her waist. Along with the oversized boots, walking proved challenging. Armed, she joined Wesley and Anden outside the camp and in the chariot. The wooden gate closed behind them as they headed out of the forest.

18

"Clear your mind," Kaylin instructed. "Concentrate on your breathing."

Victoria grew impatient meditating in the garden. Clearing her mind and focusing on nothing but her breath seemed simple in theory but difficult in practice. Thoughts and distractions buzzed around her like mosquitos pricking her mind to wander. Falling into that trap always led to an endless stream of consciousness woven by a web of thoughts meant to entangle. From her sister's safety to her father's wellbeing, they would string together until she found herself thinking of what meal sounded best for dinner. As her focus slipped, her shoulders slouched.

Next to her, Kaylin remained still with her eyes closed. "Poor posture impedes the mind."

Victoria sighed in frustration. "It doesn't matter how long I sit here. I can't do it. I can't tap into this awakening you constantly lecture about."

Her mentor's eyes fluttered open. "You wish for me to take you more seriously in sparring and use real steel, correct?"

"Of course."

"Then this is a barrier you need to break through." While firm, Kaylin's voice was comforting. "You're strong in your own right, but it's only the surface of your potential. In order to reach the furthest depths of your abilities, you need to awaken the dormant power within you." She pointed a finger at Victoria's chest. "It's there, like a fire awaiting a spark to ignite it."

Victoria had heard the same speech many times before, just decorated with different vocabulary. She hung her head, placing a hand between her breasts where Kaylin pointed. The subtle beating of her heart pulsed against her palm.

Kaylin slung an arm over Victoria's shoulder. "Don't look so glum. I know it's hard and frustrating, but you'll figure it out. Just try to be present in the current moment. Relinquish any past regrets or future concerns. Focus on the here and now."

It was banal platitude, but she knew Kaylin was trying her best. "Okay," she said. "I'll give it another try."

As Kaylin removed her arm and they prepared to return to a peaceful state of mediation, the foliage rustled as Mary Katherine forced her way through.

"Captain Gunnway," she said. "Chancellor Blackwood requires your assistance in a matter of negotiation."

Kaylin rose to her feet. "Sorry, Vic. Duty calls. Meditate for another five minutes, then call it a day." With a nod to Mary Katherine, she disappeared into the thicket of plants.

The ambassador looked down at Victoria with a soft expression. "Forgive my intrusion, Victoria."

"You saved me, actually," Victoria responded. She leaned back, resting on her arms. "Kaylin just finished another lecture."

Mary Katherine eased herself onto the grass, her dress folding over itself. "It's good to see your lessons have continued."

Along with her sister, Mary Katherine was aware of Victoria's private training with Kaylin. However, her father didn't have a clue. Being a man of diplomatic solutions, he would never allow her to practice in the ways of the sword. Ever since her mother's tragic death, the ambassador acted as a surrogate parent to her and Gwen.

"It is," said Victoria, "but recently, Kaylin's been pushing this whole meditation regimen harder than before. I hate it."

"Practicing the old traditions." A hint of curiosity laced the ambassador's words. "I've heard it's quite an intricate technique."

"More like impossible," grumbled Victoria.

"These things take time. Captain Gunnway wouldn't waste the effort teaching it to you if she thought you couldn't do it." Her face glowed in the sunlight making her smile infectious. Victoria hoped to be half as beautiful at such a mature age as Mary Katherine lay in the grass among the flower bushes like a nymph from the fables her father used to tell.

Inspired, Victoria sat forward, straightening her back. "You don't mind if I meditate, do you?"

"I'll be sure to stay quiet, as not to disturb you."

Closing her eyes, Victoria took in a deep breath, holding it for a moment before exhaling. She continued that breathing pattern as a way to maintain focus. In the darkness of her mind, an image of Gwen appeared. Her chocolate hair billowed in the wind as she strutted through an empty vacuum. Glancing over her shoulder, large hazel eyes stared at Victoria. Her face held a neutral expression, but her eyes glistened with twinkles of curiosity that doubled the number of stars across the night sky. With an exhale, her sister's image faded, dissolving into ash. This was Victoria's goal, her muse. The reason she sought strength and the skill to wield a blade. She did it for her sister so that she would not meet a similar fate as their mother.

Pressing a hand to her chest, she felt the beat of her heart again. The rhythmic thumping echoed within her head like a single melody reaching out for its other parts—a lost voice calling out into the void without a response. A touch of warmth heated her body, and she realized it was no longer her heart making the sound but something else. Faint like the embers of a dying flame. She shifted focus back to her breathing, her exhales fanning the coals to keep them lit. They glowed brighter with every breath. It was an empowering sensation, one she hoped not to lose. The sudden desperation quickened her breath enough to dash the flames. The embers faded, and the warmth turned cold.

Opening her eyes, fatigue surged throughout her body. Time escaped her, unsure whether five minutes had passed or more. Mary Katherine observed the plants around them, oblivious to what transpired. Victoria staggered to her feet. Never before had she felt this drained. The slightest touch could cause her to collapse.

"You alright?" asked the ambassador.

"Yeah," replied Victoria. "The heat must be getting to me. Think I'll head inside."

She pushed through the foliage and exited the garden as quickly as she could. Finding a secluded hall, she slid down the wall to the floor. Exhaustion took its hold. Yet, she was unsure as to why. When the warm touch faded, so did her strength. The details of the experience evaded her memory as if she had just awakened from a dream. Had a spark finally ignited the flame?

19

When the soldiers brought Walsh to Blackwood's office, the muscles in his neck strained as he yelled at the top of his lungs. After being shoved into the room, the nobleman pounded a fist against the door, demanding release. Blackwood watched him from the comfort of his desk, hands folded in his lap. Realizing no one would answer his calls, Walsh spun around.

"What is the meaning of this, Blackwood?" he spat. "As nobility, I deserve more respect than being dragged into your office like some criminal."

"Corona Borealis," said Blackwood, ignoring Walsh's outburst.

The man's angular face contorted in bewilderment. "What?"

"Corona Borealis," Blackwood repeated.

"What nonsense are you prattling on about?"

Blackwood pursed his lips and raised an eyebrow at him. "I would think someone with an interest in astronomy would recognize the name of a common constellation. Makes me wonder what you really use that telescope for if not to look at the stars."

Walsh raked the locks of his hair behind his head, revealing the icy glare of his lilac eyes. "You have no right bringing me here against my will."

"I do have the right, actually," said Blackwood. "Benefit of being chancellor is that the only ones with the power to dispute my actions are a conclave vote or the king. Unfortunately, the king is preoccupied at the moment, and I doubt a conclave would be called over the troubles of an individual such as you."

Walsh took a deep, calming breath while smoothing out the wrinkles in his tunic. "Then enlighten me, Chancellor, on why I have been brought before you."

"I've already stated it. I want to know what you look at through your telescope."

An intense pause. The noble's jowl quivered as he ground his teeth. Blackwood did not comment further. He allowed the pressure of silence to weigh heavy on Walsh until it bade him to speak.

"To be honest, it's just an antique I have lying around," he said. "As for my curiosity about astronomy, I wanted to impress you. It's not every day the Chancellor of Parliament personally pays a visit to my home."

Blackwood nodded. "Your collection of antiques is impressive. Each floor decorated with them. Interesting that your balcony, which has a gorgeous view of the palace cliffside, only has that singular one."

Walsh cleared his throat, fidgeting with the gemmed rings around his fingers. "Yes. Well, I hope to decorate my balcony with many more."

"Don't get too hopeful," said Blackwood with a mocking grin. "You see, I peered through your telescope and discovered a curious sight. Why I almost couldn't believe it."

"What did you find?" the nobleman squeaked, turning pale.

Blackwood gave him a knowing look. "I'm sure you're aware of what I saw, but if not, I have ways of jogging people's memories." He struck the wood of his desk with two sharp knocks.

His office door burst open as Kaylin Gunnway marched in and shoved the noble into a chair. Unsheathing one of her sabers, she stabbed it into the seat. Its edge pointed in the direction of his groin. Walsh melted into the back of the chair, tipping it over. The Militia captain placed a boot on the stretcher, holding it firm to the ground.

Blackwood unfolded a piece of parchment with Walsh's sigil stamped into the wax seal. "High Overseer," he read. "After refuting the summons to the palace, Chancellor Blackwood paid a visit to my home questioning on the events of the truce. While he did not press hard on the issue, I am suspicious the crown may be wise to our use of the ancient gold mines. How much they suspect me, I am unsure, but nonetheless, their investigation draws closer to unveiling the truth. Also, the whereabouts of the princess are still unknown to them. Will send word on further developments." He tossed the letter on the desk.

"Treacherous filth," growled Kaylin as she nudged the blade closer. The steel cut through the wood of the chair, nestling against the fabrics of his trousers. "Where is Guinevere? Do the rebels have her?"

The man trembled, swallowing a nervous gulp. "I — I know as much as you concerning the princess's whereabouts, I swear. As far as I know, the rebellion does not have her."

Blackwood rose from his chair and placed a firm hand on Walsh's shoulder. "What's the rebellion's plan? Their next move?"

"I don't know. I don't know. My job was to gather information on the kingdom's plans and status. That's it. The only word I receive is advised duties."

Blackwood motioned for Kaylin to sheath her blade. Pulling out a fresh piece of parchment and quill, he presented them to Walsh. "I want you to write a new letter. Tell them we don't suspect a thing and that the princess remains missing, but we are working tirelessly to find her."

The quill shook in Walsh's hand as he began to write. Blackwood watched over his shoulder, making sure it met his requirements. Once the nobleman signed his mark, Blackwood ordered the soldiers outside to take him to the dungeon. He fought and struggled, his neck straining again as they carried him out. Rolling up the parchment, Blackwood tied a thread to keep it sealed. Kaylin remained at the center of the room, tense.

"Do you think he was telling the truth?" she asked. Concern leaked into her voice. "About the rebels not having Gwen."

Blackwood returned to the seat behind his desk. "If he wasn't, we'll get the truth out of him soon enough." The hairs on his arms stood on their ends as a chill filled the room. Kaylin emitted a cold, vengeful aura.

"For their sake, they better not have taken her." A fury, unlike anything Blackwood had witnessed before, filled her eyes. It scared him. "For if they have, I'll purge the continent of anyone who dares to wrap a red band around their arm."

20

The soft impression of the Frostbitten Peaks etched itself beyond the distant haze. After days of traveling, it served as the only indication of nearing Kelveux. Anden spoke true when stating the journey from Nabal would be long. It was extended further due to increased Militia activity around Sandur, diverging them onto an indirect path. Anden and Wesley exchanged roles of piloting the chariot, allowing the other to rest in order to reach their destination faster. Gwen watched Wesley sleep in the back of the chariot.

"You both served in the Militia, didn't you?" she asked Anden. He didn't respond. "Wesley's reactions and movements were similar to Kaylin's when she fights seriously, difficult for an untrained eye to perceive. One either needs to receive REV implants or train under the old traditions to fight as he did. It also explains how you know the Burnt Coat by name."

Anden unscrewed the cap from his flask, chugging a few

gulps. "You expect me to lay out my life's story after piecing that together?"

"No," said Gwen. "Just wanting to understand why you're going through all this trouble to help me. All this effort seems worth more than thirty silver."

He glanced into the side mirror at Wesley's reflection. "I have my reasons. Luckily for you, they outweigh the annoyances you seem to bring along."

Like honey, a golden hue cascaded across the land. For once, Gwen found the dreary landscape of the countryside beautiful. They approached the edge of a river, and Anden followed along the bank.

"A branch from the Forked Tongue," he said. "Kelveux rests at the crest where the two branches meet. Means we're not too far out." The chariot sputtered and coughed, slowing in speed before stopping completely. Anden punched the wheel. "Dammit."

Wesley jerked awake. "What's going on?"

"Out of fuel," Anden groaned, "and we don't have any left in the canister, so we'll have to walk. There should be a hunter outpost in the town. Hopefully, they might have some to spare."

Gwen hesitated to leave. "You're just going to leave it here? In the middle of nowhere?"

"Hardly anyone travels to the Forked Tongue, and no beasts will take an interest. The old girl doesn't have any meat on her," Anden answered.

Reluctantly, Gwen hopped out of the chariot with her sword fastened to her hip. The three of them continued along the riverbank as daylight faded.

The night was feral in Kelveux, which was less of a town and more of a graveyard. Screeches and howls filled the void of silence upon entering. The remaining buildings were abandoned and dilapidated, housing forgotten tokens left by their former occupants. The light of a full moon revealed gashes in the wood and stains of blood that told stories of slaughter. Gwen gripped the hilt of her blade as invisible eyes watched them in the dark. Whether it was the ghosts of those killed or the monsters who killed them, it was equally unsettling.

Anden led the way through the deserted streets to a stone well covered by a thick, metal door. A wheel, similar to the one used to steer the chariot, was fastened to it. Anden twisted it, and with a metallic groan, the door opened to a claustrophobic descent down a ladder. Wesley entered first, followed by Gwen, then Anden, who slammed the door shut. The darkness forced Gwen to rely on her body's innate rhythm for finding each rung of the ladder. She slipped on a few steps but kept her grip and made the climb down.

Two lanterns hung on either side of a door. Anden provided a solid knock, and a slot slid open, revealing a stern pair of eyes.

"What do you want?" a voice grumbled.

"Seeking refuge for the night," said Anden.

The stranger's gaze passed over each of them. "Don't look like hunters. Strange for common folk to pass through this part of the continent."

Anden slid two silver coins through the slot. "Looking for a hunter and got word we might find him here."

The slot slid shut, and the door opened. The stranger behind was a hefty set man with dark skin like Wesley's and a scar ripping across his face. "You'll want to talk to Jarah." He nodded them into a room constructed like the lobby of an inn. A handful of hunters crowded the tables, coated in scars. Some even had mechanical prosthetic limbs. "Hey, Jarah, got some people here to talk to ya."

A woman with a patch over her left eye poked her head in from another room. One side held long locks of red hair while the other was shaved bald. "Looks like new blood. Take a seat. I'll be with you in a moment."

They took their seats as her head popped back into the room. Ten minutes passed before she joined them. Unlike the hunters up north, she didn't wear the typical pelts or furs. Instead, two metal pauldrons sat on her shoulders, and a dirty tank top covered her lithe torso.

"That's some fine equipment you're hauling," she commented, noting their weapons. "You're not hunters or Militia, and you don't seem to be sporting a stripe anywhere.

You mercs of some kind?"

"Pretty much," said Wesley. "We're looking for a hunter by the name of Damian Briggs. A bookkeeper up north told us his last job was in this area."

Jarah scoffed. "Did they?" She offered a doleful look. One that typically expressed bad news. "Let me get you something to drink before we continue. It's our own bootlegged brew, but it's better than nothing."

Anden and Wesley accepted her offer, but Gwen politely declined. The hunter returned carrying three tankards foaming with a strange, green tonic. Wesley sniffed his before taking a drink. Anden downed two hearty gulps without a second thought.

Jarah wiped her lips clean, having already finished half of her drink. "When I heard tales that the Burnt Coat joined the Core, I wasn't sure whether or not to believe it. That was until he came marching in here one day looking for contracts. Man hunts those demons like his life depends on it, or rather like he has a life worth losing."

"Is he still here in Kelveux?" asked Anden.

Jarrah's finger traced the rim of her tankard. "I'm not usually one to prod people on their business, but why do you need the Burnt Coat? Plenty of other hunters around who will do any job that pays well."

"We're in need of someone with a specific skill set," explained Anden, "and he meets it. So, is he here or not?"

Jarah lifted the tankard to her mouth, finishing the rest of her drink. "There's been a bolgia prowling around preying on us. Those who have survived an encounter with the beast claim it's massive and nigh invincible with horns as long as a broadsword and claws like daggers. That didn't stop him. He took the contract and headed out to hunt the creature on his own. Few days have passed since then."

"Do you think he's dead?" asked Gwen. She would hate to have come all this way to find a corpse. Not to mention it foiled their plans for sneaking into Danforth.

"I can't say for certain, but it wouldn't shock me."

Anden slammed his tankard onto the table, the green liquid spilling over. "I won't believe Damian's dead. Not unless I see it for myself."

Jarah shook her head. "I'm sure you've come across a fleshling horde or two, but bolgias are entirely different creatures. Even skilled hunters hesitate to take them on."

Wesley finished his drink, slamming his tankard down as well. "We've faced more than our fair share of monsters. We can handle ourselves."

"You might, but the girl can't." Jarah pointed a finger at Gwen. "I can tell she's never swung a sword in her life. Sending her out there is a death sentence."

"Then she can stay here," said Anden. "Surely, you have beds."

"This isn't an inn," snapped the hunter. She looked over at

Gwen, who sat in her chair, frightened. She thought about the bolgia Johnny mentioned at their first meeting. The one in the estuaries that would drown people. This monster that Jarah described seemed worse. Recognizing her fear, the hunter took pity and relented. "However, since you two seem to be just as crazy as the Burnt Coat, I'll allow it. Just know that if you die, she'll be stranded here, alone."

Anden turned to her with his copper eyes. Looking into them under the brim of his hat, she could see they were filled with confidence. Something made him believe they would survive. "Stay here and rest. Might be a while before we find Damian."

"Just don't die." She glanced over at Wesley. "Either of you."

Wesley's mouth stretched into a toothy grin. "Don't worry. I'll make sure this bastard doesn't get us killed."

With that, they sauntered out the door, leaving Gwen alone with Jarah.

"Come on," she said, standing from the table, "I'll show you to the barracks."

Gwen followed her into a hall with rows of beds lining the walls. Thin, woolen sheets covered the stiff mattresses made from straw. Gwen chose one at the far end of the room, resting her head on the pillow. It held little comfort, but exhaustion overwhelmed her. As she closed her eyes, she whispered a prayer for the First Emperor to hear. She prayed for the safe return of her companions along with the Burnt Coat. All of them still alive.

21

The converging river of the Forked Tongue snaked a path leading into the Demons' Cavity, but Anden hoped their search wouldn't take them so far. Only fools seeking glory in empty claims journeyed into such a wasteland, and Damian wasn't one of them. A foul stench tainted the air as he and Wesley trod along the riverbank. The smell of death was common in this region, but this smell was a wet, soggy death like a fish flopped ashore and its carcass laid bare for weeks. Something snapped under Wesley's foot, a bone covered in tatters of decomposed skin. The claws at the end of the fingers helped them identify it as a fleshling limb. Inspecting the rest of the area, they discovered more body parts littered about—remains of a slaughtered horde. The cuts severing the limbs were clean.

"This is Damian's handiwork if I've ever seen it," said Wesley.

Anden agreed. Damian's signature in the artform of killing was hacking any unfortunate soul who crossed his blade with a single stroke. The only one who arguably could match his strength was Balavan Winter, another Militia captain.

"Anden, over here," Wesley called out. He squatted near the outskirts of the massacre, rubbing a finger on the ground. "Got a small trail of blood. Fleshling might've nicked him."

The blood was dry, having been spilled hours or days ago. The trail directed them toward a small camp far from the riverbank. Charred fleshling limbs smoldered in a pile.

"Coals are still warm," said Wesley, holding a hand over the embers.

Anden sat next to the makeshift firepit. His legs ached after relieving them from his weight. The constant walking throughout the day started taking its toll. "We should wait out the night and see if he returns. If we continue wandering aimlessly, we may miss him."

Wesley joined him, lying flat on the ground and gazing into the sky. "We gonna take shifts or just not sleep at all?"

"I don't think I can sleep right now," said Anden. "Not in this place."

"I don't think I can either. That encounter back at Nabal still has me shaken. We need to be wary of whoever or whatever that thing was because I don't think it's alone."

"What do you mean?" asked Anden.

"Before it disappeared, it said it was told not to stir up too much commotion. Meaning there's probably more of them out there, and they have a leader." His dark face blended with the night turning his eyes into floating orbs reflecting the ember's glow. "If they want the princess, we'll need to tread carefully and keep our eyes open. I'd hate to encounter more than one of those things."

"All the more reason to find Damian and haul our asses to Danforth," said Anden. He didn't want to admit to his own fear. After seeing the state Wesley was in after fighting one of those cloaked figures, the possibility of more existing terrified him.

They stayed awake, watching the glow of the pit dim. The passage of time was fleeting as it neither grew darker nor lighter. Crickets chattered, filling the void of conversation. Anden and Wesley waited. A howl pierced the night air forcing them to their feet. A beastly shroud ambled toward them, standing erect on its back haunches like a man but towering twice as high. Two horns crowned its head as two yellow slits glared at them. Wesley instinctively unloaded a few shots at the creature. The bullets ricocheted off its hide, thick as iron. Anden charged, swinging his weapon into its knees. With a massive talon, it flung him across the campsite, leaving a deep gash in his chest. Wesley fired more shots; however, in a single bound, the beast pinned him to the ground and bared its fangs.

Anden struggled to stand as the blow left him winded and bloodied.

"Here, beast!" A stranger waved a torch. The flame danced over his head, catching the creature's attention.

Releasing Wesley, it charged toward the stranger, galloping on all fours. As it neared him, the stranger tossed the torch into the creature's snout, blinding it. He dodged and unsheathed his blade, the steel kissed by a faint teardrop of moonlight. Before he could strike, its tail whipped around and knocked him flat on his back. The beast lumbered toward him, primed for the kill.

The crack of another gunshot sent the creature wailing, as one of its yellow eyes exploded in a stream of black blood. Wesley lay on the ground, arm tucked under the barrel of his pistol. Back on his feet, the stranger grasped his sword and severed one of the beast's horns from its head with a mighty swing. Wounded, the creature fled into the wasteland.

Feeling dizzy, Anden stumbled forward and collapsed to the ground. His chest was warm with blood and stung with immense pain. Through his blurred vision, he saw two figures standing over him. One of them pulled out a sword and held a flame in their hand. He ran it along the length of the blade until the steel held the heat and pressed the blunt end against the wound. The searing of his flesh burned, and Anden's body fought the pain, but Wesley held him down. With the hot steel removed, he still felt the lingering heat and his vision cleared.

Anden recognized the blade, a bastard sword crafted from the finest metal on the continent with a guard on the handle curving inward like a crescent moon. Through the mask of blood and dirt, he also recognized the face of the man wielding it.

"Of all the places," said Damian." What are you two doing here? We agreed never to see each other again. To disappear."

"Circumstances have changed, unfortunately," said Wesley.

Anden sat up, wincing in pain. "Good to see you're still alive."

"You still haven't answered my question," Damian scolded. "What are you doing here?"

Wesley picked up the severed horn on the ground. It was about the length of a dagger and just as sharp. "We came looking for you."

Damian snatched the horn from Wesley and tucked it into his sheepskin coat. "It better be for a good reason seeing you went through the trouble of tracking me down all the way out here." Years serving as a captain of the Militia equipped Damian with an intimidating presence and gave his voice a harsh tone.

Wesley helped Anden to his feet. "The reasons for our gatherings in the past were never good," Anden jested.

"Just spit it out," demanded Damian.

Wesley exchanged a glance with Anden before speaking. "No sense in beating around the bush. We need your help getting into Danforth."

Damian's stern, gray eyes met them with silence. Sheathing his sword, he turned his back to them and marched off into the night.

"Where are you going?" asked Wesley.

Damian kept walking. "To hunt down that bolgia. I have no interest in returning to Danforth, and neither should you."

"We haven't told you why we need to go to Danforth," Anden added. "We're helping the royal heir herself, Lady Guinevere Clougher."

Damian rounded on Anden, seizing his torn tunic. All that filled Anden's vision was the cold gaze and wrinkled brow of the former Militia captain. "Have you two lost your minds?" he raved. "The whole point of us splitting up was to not be hunted by the Militia and fade into obscurity. You might as well be holding a beacon for the kingdom to find you. Do you have a death wish?"

Anden shoved himself free from Damian's grasp. "Speak for yourself. The hunters stationed here told us of your exploits. They think you're mad, and that's saying something. Killing a thousand of these demons won't bring your men back. It won't erase the past."

"And helping you get into Danforth somehow will?"

Anden curled his hands into fists, veins protruding from his forearms. "It could be a start. This is the princess we're talking about. She's heir to the throne and will one day possess the power to absolve us from our crimes. If we help her now, we have leverage later on. We won't have to hide anymore, separated and alone."

Damian's hard face softened with grief. "Too many years have gone by. I'm with the Core now. My duty is to send these dark spawns back to whatever hell they came from. I'm sorry." Turning away, he followed in the direction the creature had fled.

Wesley placed a comforting hand on Anden's shoulder and offered a reassuring smile. "How about we help you hunt this bolgia?" he said to Damian. "Give you some time to reconsider."

Damian paused, glancing over his shoulder. "I guess it's never a bad idea to have some help."

The cold wind cut through skin and rattled bones as they ventured deeper into the wasteland. It wasn't long before they discovered a trail of large footprints leading to the base of a small mound, where they faded into the darkness of a cave. Damian removed a metallic cylinder from his jacket. Sticking a vial of liquid into it, he flicked his finger, and a small flame ignited. With the flickering light fighting back the shadows, they entered a tunnel narrowed by stalagmites. A threshold awaited them at the end and beyond that was an expansive cavern littered with bones. Near the back wall, the bolgia rubbed its stump of a horn against the stone, groaning. Preoccupied, it didn't notice them enter its lair. Damian fished out another clear vial of liquid. Reflected in the firelight, Anden recognized it to be gasoline.

"I'll lay a trail of gas and get its attention," Damian explained. He motioned toward a small ridge lining the wall. "Anden, you get some high ground. When I give the signal, Wesley sets the gas ablaze, and Anden mounts the beast to restrain it. That should give me a clear shot to kill it."

"Sounds good," said Wesley. "Not like my bullets can do much against its hide."

Anden sneaked over to the ridge, careful not to step on any bones. Pulling himself up the wall stone by stone, his fingers and toes dug hard into the small crevices between them. Wesley remained near the cavern's entrance holding the flame as Damian poured a line of gas between him and the creature. Once Anden perched himself on the ridge, he signaled to Damian, who unsheathed his sword. The hum of the blade drew the creature's singular yellow eye onto him. Lowering to all fours, it recklessly charged.

"Now," Damian ordered.

Wesley lit the trail of gasoline, sprouting a wall of flames. The sudden fire frightened the bolgia into rearing back. Anden leaped from the ridge onto the beast, jammed the center rod of his three-section staff into its mouth, and used the other two rods as reins. The bolgia tried to buck him off, the rough texture of its hide rubbing against the scar on his chest. It reignited the pain, but Anden held firm. Damian emerged from the fire with his blade aimed to pierce the creature's chest but was thwarted again by its tail whipping him to the ground.

The bolgia slammed its body into the wall, cracking the stone. It took two blows for Anden to lose his grip and fall. Spitting out the weapon in a clatter of chains, it reared its head toward him before unleashing a howl of pain as Damian managed to hack off its slithering tail. The beast lunged at him, forcing him against the opposite wall and digging its sharp horn into his side. Damian vomited blood as the horn dug deeper. Grabbing his weapon, Anden raced to Damian's aid but was knocked away by the bolgia's back leg. His body ached as he tried to stumble forward to save his friend.

Wesley tossed the small torch device. It hurtled through the air toward the bolgia's flank, and with a single shot, exploded into a scorching ball of fire. Flinching, the creature released Damian, freeing its horn from his side. Anden wrapped his chains around the bolgia's horn in an attempt to restrain it. Wesley joined him in holding the panicked creature at bay. It lashed and shook, fearful and desperate to escape their grasp. Picking up his sword, Damian thrust it into the beast's skull, and with a twist, the body went limp.

The cave went silent. Only the sounds of Anden and Wesley's heavy breathing echoed within the cavern. Damian collapsed into a scarlet pool of his own blood. The gaping hole in his side could prove fatal if not directly treated. Anden and Wesley scooped him up over their shoulder and carried him out of the cave.

His strength faded, making his voice a whisper. "You can't just let me die, can you?"

Anden gave a brazen smirk. "Never, you son of a bitch."

22

Holding the intercepted letter from Walsh, the king rubbed his eyes in sorrow. Blackwood sat in a chair next to the king's bed, patiently waiting for Peter to process everything. He skimmed it over several times before speaking. "This madness will never end, and Walsh made no mention of my daughter?"

"He claims not to know anything regarding her whereabouts," said Blackwood. "Kaylin nearly beat the noble to death in the dungeon, believing he was withholding such information, yet he offered nothing." Blackwood looked at his friend with dread and remorse. "It's been days since even a rumor of a sighting has reached our ears. The continent is vast. She could be anywhere…"

"Speak no more, Blackwood." In his meager state, the king could still add a harsh sting to his words. "I will not stop searching for my daughter as long as I draw breath. Do you understand?"

"Yes, Your Majesty." Like any father, the king would tear the continent apart piece by piece if it meant finding his daughter. "In regard to the rebels, we should act in some way. The truce is nothing but a farce, a veil draped over our eyes while they continue to scheme. We cannot allow it."

Peter closed his eyes, deep in thought. His bony, wrinkled body lay motionless in the bed like a fresh cadaver. He was frail, nothing like the man he was many days ago when he stood against an assassin sent to kill him. "We should let the illusion last," he said.

Blackwood leaned out of the chair, eyes wide with shock. "What do you mean let it last? Do nothing?"

The king calmly turned to Blackwood flashing his brilliant blue orbs. "It is not certain whether or not the rebellion has my daughter. If they do and we mount an open attack, I have no doubt they'll use her as a form of retaliation. We need to be discreet. Besides, the kingdom hasn't shared a peace like this for many, many years. Is it so bad to entertain a dream for a moment, knowing it isn't real?"

Blackwood buried his face into his hands. Pulling away, he slid off the chair, standing. "Peter, I'm willing to stand with you, but the other ambassadors will not be content in remaining idle. As far as they're concerned, you still have another daughter to inherit the crown upon your death."

"Call a conclave," said the king, unperturbed. "Allow them to deliberate and decide what our next course of action should be. It is a matter concerning the entire kingdom."

Blackwood's head hung low on his shoulders. He despised conclaves. Nothing more than glorified altercations between inflated egos. Constant debate and arguments for days on end, and him at the center, moderating it all. It was inescapable. If Peter didn't command him to call one, the ambassadors would surely do so.

He took the letter from the king, holding a bony hand in his own. "As you wish." He strode out of the king's chambers into the torch-lit halls where soldiers stood guard. Blackwood waited until he was out of sight to lean against a wall and allow his soul to shatter. He felt torn between his duty as chancellor and responsibility as a friend. What was best for Peter as a father may not be best for the kingdom. The coming days, months even, would prove the most trying time in his career. How would he emerge—a faithful servant to the people or a loyal friend to his king?

23

A sudden commotion shook Gwen awake. Jarah and some other hunters crowded around a singular bed. Blood tarnished the sheets as the female hunter pulled her fiery head of hair into a tail while shouting for medical supplies. Through a gap in the crowd, Gwen saw an unconscious man with a massive gash in his side. The hole was large enough to fit her whole hand through. It was a miracle for him not to be dead. Once the medical supplies arrived, Jarah tended to the wound, trying to stop the bleeding. Out by the bar, Wesley uncorked a bottle and poured a drink. He handed it to Anden, who winced as he reached for the glass. His tunic was torn down the middle, unveiling fresh scar tissue covering his chest. Dirt and blood splattered across their clothes and skin, and fatigue weighed on their bodies.

She rushed over to Anden and lightly touched the scar on his chest. "What happened?"

He recoiled in pain as the tips of her fingers grazed it. "Nothing to fret about. I'm fine."

"Emperor be praised. Once Jarah finishes tending to the man bleeding out, she should check on you two." She studied Wesley's bandages which were discolored, and the threads unraveled along the fringes. "Who is that man anyway?"

"That," explained Wesley, "is the Burnt Coat himself."

Gwen glanced back at the doorway to the barracks, where painful groans emanated. "Do you think he'll make it?"

"He better fucking make it," said Anden. "Otherwise, I'm going to beat the shit out of his corpse with my own hands."

Jarah exited the barracks wiping her arms with a rag. The blood stained her forearms pink. "I was able to stop the bleeding and cover the wound. He should make it, albeit by a thread."

"Appreciate the help," said Wesley, offering her a drink.

The hunter declined with a wave of her hand. "You managed to bring that crazy bastard back and kill the bolgia. The damn thing left a hell of a parting gift."

"How long do you think it'll be before he's fit to travel?" asked Anden.

Jarah freed her hair, allowing it to drape over one of her pauldrons. "Hard to say. Tough fellow like him, maybe a couple of days or more."

Anden lumbered past her toward the hall of beds. "Since he's stable, I'm going to hit the hay."

"I second that," said Wesley, finishing his drink and following close behind.

Jarah watched them with intrigue. "Those mercs of yours are tougher than they seem."

A smile forced itself onto Gwen's lips as she cleaned up their glasses. "Yeah, they sure are."

Word quickly spread throughout the outpost of the bolgia's death. Hunters celebrated with drinks, songs, and fables of the battle leading to its demise. No one knew the truth, of course, except for Anden, Wesley, and the Burnt Coat, who all slept in the other room. Gwen checked on their condition throughout the day, watching them rest. Hours passed, and none of them showed any sign of waking. Anden sprawled out across the bed, the green sheet barely covering his body. Wesley slept on his side, his bandages removed. Most of the gashes healed, some leaving faint scars. The Burnt Coat lay on the flat of his back. His appearance wasn't at all what she expected. The tales described him as a lunatic, but looking at him lost in the serenity of sleep reminded her more of the old knights depicted in stories before the Battle of Brothers. He had wavy locks of ashen hair, and hard lines defined his clean-shaven face giving him a chiseled jaw. Even unconscious, he seemed stoic. At the foot of his bed rested a long sword about a foot shorter than

Gwen from handle to tip. Staring at it sheathed, she wondered if it was the same sword used to kill his men all those years ago.

He awakened from his slumber with a small cough. Gwen rushed to his bedside as his eyes barely opened. Through his hazed vision, he looked up at Gwen's hovering face. He stared at her for a long moment with his dull, gray eyes. It was like he recognized her but was unsure from where. His lips parted to speak, only to close again as he sank back into an unconscious state.

Anden was the first to wake and promptly sought Jarah asking about fuel for the chariot. She handed him a canister along with a sack of coins for slaying the bolgia. Wesley awoke shortly after, and the two spent their time accepting congratulations and telling the other hunters how they killed the creature. Gwen had no interest in listening and instead sat in the bed next to the Burnt Coat. He hadn't moved or showed any signs of consciousness since that brief moment hours ago. She hadn't mentioned it to anyone either.

Jarah offered her a warm cup of tea. "He still out cold?"

"Yeah," she said, taking a sip. It was bitter.

Jarah lifted the sheet and inspected the wound. She managed to stitch it closed and applied a rubbing alcohol to

avoid infection. Covering him up, she left Gwen to drink her
tea and continue observing his condition. Anden and Wesley
both came to check on him as well. Wesley joined her on the
bed while Anden stood over the Burnt Coat.

"After he wakes up," she said, "how do you plan on getting
us into Danforth?"

"Damian knows of a secret entrance into the city,"
explained Anden. "He'll guide us through it and get us in.
From there, it's the homestretch to Noreen."

"Hopefully, he wakes soon." Gwen hugged her legs to her
chest. "The sooner we leave here, the better." Death had a
certain hold on this place, sending a shiver down her spine.

"I'm right there with you," agreed Anden.

They remained by the Burnt Coat's bedside for some time
until boredom drew Wesley and Anden back out to the bar.
Gwen finished her cup of tea and set it aside on a nearby table.
Her body felt weak as she lay on the bed and closed her eyes.
So much of her day was spent anxiously waiting for the Burnt
Coat to wake that she'd lost track of time. She fell asleep for a
short while, just enough to regain some strength. Opening her
eyes, she grabbed the empty cup from the bedside table and
headed for the door to return it to the bar. The moan of a
mattress stopped her in her tracks. Standing from the bed was
the Burnt Coat, clutching his side where the wound healed.
Shocked, she dropped the teacup, sending it shattering to the
floor.

The Burnt Coat's gaze snapped to Gwen, and grabbing his blade, he lumbered toward her using it as a crutch. Hearing the sound of the shattering cup, Anden, Wesley, and Jarah raced through the doorway. Gwen remained paralyzed as he shambled closer. Her head met his chest as he stood before her. Dropping to one knee, he held the blade in front of him, pointed downward.

"My lady," he said calmly, "though the nights may be dark and the days uncertain, I pledge my service to you. Your will guides my sword until you require my strength no longer or I draw my last breath. With permission, I stand to aid and protect you."

Gwen was taken aback by such action. He invoked the Vow of Sanction, a pledge King Edward's Seven Saints recited to affirm their service and loyalty. It was an olive branch asking her if she trusted him to be by her side. She could decline, and a part of her wanted to as trust withers in the hands of traitors, but according to Anden, they couldn't get into Danforth without his help.

She raised her chin, looking down with her hazel eyes. "Granted," she said.

Pulling himself to his feet, he bowed his head. Lifting his eyes, he stared at Anden and Wesley standing behind her. Confusion transfixed their faces, unaware of what just took place. "We should be on our way," he said. "We've wasted enough time lounging about."

Jarah stepped forward, scolding him, "You're not fully recovered yet."

The Burnt Coat threw on his shirt and jacket, strapping his sword across his back. "You did a fine job of patching me up. I can rest more after we hit the road."

The female hunter sighed, shaking her head. She knew it was futile to try and argue. Gathering their supplies, they left the outpost and trekked back to the mechanical chariot. It rested along the riverbank where they had left it. As Anden and Wesley said, the pile of scraps remained untouched. Anden refilled the tank beneath the front seat, and with a loud rumble, they headed off to Danforth.

24

The noise of shouting orders and sprinting footsteps penetrated the fabrics of Reed's tent as she packed necessary provisions. In the past few days, little time existed to sit with her own thoughts and stroll her spot on the hillside—too much work needed to be done. Supplies needed gathering, and troops needed rallying. Everything seemed to be coming together, except Vargo was still missing. No word came in from the assassin or the spy watching him. Reed's concern grew as they could not afford to keep waiting. The sooner they struck, the better. Opening a small chest, she took out a set of twin daggers. The small blades curved into an ebony handle laced with silver. Strategy and leadership weren't the only skills her uncle had taught her before passing. When this war was over, the blood of the royal family would drip down their steel. She slid them into the sheath strapped to her lower back.

Elliot Durham pushed through the entryway. "Watts says preparations will be complete in time for departure first thing tomorrow."

"Good," she said, latching her leather case shut. "Any word on the whereabouts of the princess?"

"None." He rubbed a hand over his bald head. "It's been nearly a week since her last sighting. She's most likely dead by this point."

"Let's hope so." She tossed the case onto the table and sat in her chair, kicking up her feet. "And Vargo?"

Elliot frowned at the mention of the assassin. "Nothing on that front either. He's been too quiet." Her high overseer sat as well, resting an elbow on the table. "Perhaps it's a blessing in disguise for that… man to not rejoin our efforts."

Reed noted Elliot's hesitance to call Vargo a man. She had to agree. Two REV implants could decrease a person's lifespan by half from the number of toxins pumping throughout their body. Rumors from the underground stated the assassin underwent four and somehow lived if one wished to call it that. On one occasion, she glimpsed under the assassin's hood to see a mask of decayed flesh.

A rhythmic clanking of metal grew louder as the flap of her tent flew open. Vargo Vasallo stepped in, holding a burlap sack reeking of death with flies orbiting around it. Reed kept her feet aloft while Elliot rose from his chair in a defiant stance with his chest puffed out.

"Are you always tardy upon being summoned," said Reed, "or do you save that honor for us?"

The assassin turned the sack over, dumping out the disembodied head of the spy they sent to watch him. It rolled onto the table with pale skin and milky, white eyes similar to Vargo's. They stared at Reed, empty.

"I stumbled across one of your men on my travels," hissed the assassin. "He may have just gotten lost, but one can never be too careful." He gave a sideways glance to Elliot, who stared at the head, unsettled.

"An unfortunate accident," Reed said coldly. "Just make sure it doesn't happen again."

"As long as they don't interfere with my work, it shouldn't be a problem." He paced the length of the table, running a hand over the spot where the map once lay. "Fearsome contraption you've managed to build. It seems the years and resources were well spent."

Reed's emerald gaze followed him as he approached her end of the table. "You'll witness it in action firsthand. We head out first thing in the morning. I expect you to be ready."

He rubbed a thumb over his fingers. "And how much payment is to be expected from helping you win this war of yours?"

Reed lowered her feet from the table and fished out a small purse from her trousers, tossing it to the assassin. He opened it, checking the amount of coin. "Similar to our prior arrangement," she said, "you'll get half now and half when the job is done."

Satisfied, he pocketed the purse and drifted out of the tent, leaving the severed head on the table. Elliot picked up the burlap sack and gently placed it over the head, covering it.

"Damn him, but it was foolish to assume any other outcome," Elliot said in disgust.

"Apparently so," said Reed. "You're dismissed as well."

Elliot took his leave, thankful to get away from the putrid stench.

Reed rose from her chair and scooped up the head inside the sack. On her way out of the tent, she grabbed a shovel and climbed the hill to her usual spot overlooking the western sea. Shoveling the soil, she dug a hole. Not too wide or deep. It only needed to hold a head. It was a shame for one of their own to die in such a merciless manner. Although, there was no one to blame but herself, which is why she took on the responsibility to bury the remains. The sound of the crashing waves carried by the wind reached the top of the hill as she placed the head into the hole.

Packing the dirt back in, Reed muttered the rebellion's creed as an obituary for the fallen soldier. "We wear the blood of fallen brothers spilled to nourish the phoenix's ashes. While its feathers appear lush and beautiful, its talons strike down all without mercy. The sins of the father must be rectified despite whose head wears the crown."

25

Ever since the surreal experience of meditating next to Mary Katherine in the garden, Victoria chased the feeling of the warm touch. She no longer loathed meditating, instead practicing multiple times a day following her sessions with Kaylin. Her private chambers served as the perfect place for such a ritual as anyone rarely disturbed her. She sat cross-legged, leaning against the bed as it assisted in keeping her back straight. She replicated the pattern of breathing, a deep inhale followed by a brief pause before exhaling. The rhythm of her beating heart was all she focused on, expecting to hear the melody once more. It never came. The day passed, and Victoria scarcely moved. The growl of hunger broke her concentration. Evening approached, and so did the time for supper. With little progress to be made on an empty stomach, Victoria left her chambers and descended the lengthy stairwell.

Wading through the ornate halls, she passed by the door to Mary Katherine's quarters.

"Surely, you realize the foolishness of holding a conclave to debate such a matter," a voice said. "We have evidence supporting the rebellion hired the assassin, and we should respond swiftly by swarming the estuaries with our forces and pull the rebellion out root and all."

Victoria recognized the voice of Mary Katherine. "And what will it accomplish?" she spoke in a harsh tone. "First Richard, then Boris, now Reed. Killing their leaders does nothing except create martyrs to rally more people to their cause, and the king has a point. We don't know whether or not they have Gwen. This situation needs to be handled delicately with diplomacy."

Victoria peeked through the slit in the door to see a husky individual with tanned skin sitting across from Mary Katherine. Anger made her face more rigid, showing her age. A glint of light reflected from the man's spectacles. Along with the dark, raven-colored hair, she recognized him to be Ambassador Rahm Krawczyk. With a conclave being called, he and Ambassador Fletcher were the first to arrive.

"While we debate, the rebels have more time to adapt whatever scheme they hope to put in motion," said Krawczyk. "We cannot allow the fate of the entire kingdom to rest on the possibility that they hold one of the girls hostage. Even so, if the worse is to come, the king has another daughter."

Mary Katherine pointed a finger at him with wild eyes. "Don't you dare say such things in front of me."

"I'm not the only one who thinks this way. Parson and Brookshire share my concerns."

"Why come to me then?" she asked. "Assuming Fletcher is in your pocket as usual and considering you can buy Weyman's vote, what need is there to convince me?"

The large man's chair creaked as he leaned back in it. "Fletcher is timid, but I'm sure he'll come around. As for Weyman, that weasel will play his games to try and bleed me of as much coin as he can. This needs to be settled quickly, with a single vote. Otherwise, who knows what the repercussions of our inaction will be. I know the king and, therefore, the chancellor wish to seek a diplomatic resolution, but that requires our opposition to share the desire for such an outcome. We both know that's not the case."

Mary Katherine folded her arms over her chest in a steadfast manner. "What you're suggesting is genocide at the possible cost of Gwen's life. Nothing will be gained from it. Even if you do uproot the entire rebellion, the people will live in fear of us."

"Fear is power," said Krawczyk with conviction. "Power garners respect. How can we hope to maintain any semblance of peace if our power is not respected?"

She shook her head. "I won't."

Ambassador Krawczyk rose from his chair and adjusted his spectacles. "I hoped you'd see reason, but it seems emotions continue to cloud your judgment. Perhaps the conclave will dissipate those illusions. Pray the rebels don't use our time squabbling amongst ourselves to strike."

Turning away, he marched toward the door. Victoria dashed around the corner as it opened. The ambassador slammed the door shut behind him and stomped down the hall with his heavy feet, mumbling angrily to himself. Victoria watched him leave, and as he turned the corner, she continued down the hall to the kitchen. It was shocking to hear that the rebels were the ones to make an attempt on her father's life and that they may possibly have her sister. If the war were to reignite, she was certain nothing good would come of it.

She crossed the threshold of the giant oak doors into the Great Hall. Clusters of people gathered around the tables feasting on their supper. Those she passed gave a respectful bow as she strode straight toward the kitchen. Upon entering, the clatter of kitchenware reverberated off the walls, and a mixture of smells permeated the air. Artemis, a hound nearly the size of a pony, bounded up to her. She bent down to pet him as the dog slapped its meaty tongue across her cheek, coating it in saliva. While Artemis looked like the type of beast to rip a man's arm off, he was a gentle creature.

Madness consumed the rest of the kitchen. Cooks sprinted from one station to the next, preparing ingredients, grabbing utensils, and washing used dishes. From the outside, everything seemed like chaos, but there existed a flow to it all. Every move was coordinated. The head chef, Helmond, wove through the pandemonium without hitting a single person.

"Artemis," the chef said, "what is with the commotion?" He froze for a moment seeing Victoria and quickly bowed. His crimson ponytail fell over his shoulder. "Milady, please excuse me. I did not know you were coming."

He spoke in a vernacular commonly found in towns around the frozen tundra near the base of the Frostbitten Peaks. Instead of addressing nobles as my lady or my lord, they streamed the words into one.

"It's alright, Helmond," said Victoria. "I was struck by a pang of hunger and figured I'd come visit you and Arty."

The hound sat next to her, its tail sweeping the floor.

Helmond twirled the end of his mustache. "Artemis's favorite visitor is always welcomed. What are you craving, Lady Victoria?"

"Whatever you make, I'll eat."

With a genuflect, he shuffled back into the bustling mass of bodies. While the head chef prepared a delicious concoction, Victoria returned to petting Artemis. His brindle coat was soft to the touch, and he enjoyed her playing with his floppy ears. When his tongue hung out of his snout, he wore a funny-looking smile of endless joy. Victoria formed a bond with the hound that Helmond couldn't help but notice. She could journey through every hall within the palace, and Artemis would never leave her side. Helmond returned carrying two plates decorated with pieces of fish resting on a bed of asparagus and tomatoes.

"The fish just came in from the coasts of Papuri," he said. "Supposed to be a real delicacy." He handed both plates to her with a somber expression. "I made a plate for your father as well. He hardly comes down to the Great Hall anymore, and I can't keep track if he actually eats a sufficient amount every day. He shouldn't skip any meals, especially at his age."

Victoria nodded, taking the plates of food. Bidding farewell to the head chef and Artemis, she left the kitchen for her father's chambers. Little of her father was seen by anyone since Gwen's disappearance. He either spent his days locked up in his chambers or brooding in the throne room. Those who had seen him said he looked ill and malnourished. Candlelight guided her to her father's chambers, where a pair of Militia soldiers stood guard. Recognizing her, they allowed her in.

Her father rested on the bed gazing out the arched window overlooking the city. Helmond was right to be concerned. He was thin and ravaged with grief. His garments wrapped loosely around his frail figure.

She spoke softly, "Father, I brought you some supper."

Two brilliant blue orbs shifted their gaze from the window to her. "Thank you, my dear. It seems my thoughts distracted my stomach from realizing how hungry it is." He noticed the second plate in her hand. "I see you haven't eaten either. Would you care to join me?"

Victoria climbed into the bed next to her father. They each dug into their food, silverware clinking against the plates. Her father ate at a slower pace, carefully cutting the fish while Victoria scarfed it down.

"There's yet to be a dish Helmond could not cook to perfection," he commented with his mouth full.

"You should pay him a visit and tell him that," suggested Victoria. "I'm sure he'd appreciate the sentiment."

The fork shook in her father's hand as he lifted it for another bite. "I do not wish to disturb him. He will be very busy in the coming days. Many mouths to feed as the ambassadors gather."

"What do you expect the outcome of the conclave to be?"

The question stole her father's appetite from him as he set down the utensils. "I expect them to come to some sort of a conclusion as they always do," he said bluntly.

"And what if they decide to redeclare war on the rebellion? Will you adhere to their decision with the possibility of them keeping Gwen hostage?"

His expression hardened. Despite his disheveled state, he could still put on the face of the king. "Parliament will debate on the political matters of the continent. The world does not stop because we will it. I will search into the heart of the Demons' Cavity and beyond the Frostbitten Peaks for your sister. With luck, the rebels aren't the ones who have captured her, and we can safely bring her home without issue. In the meantime, the realm cannot simply be ignored."

"You didn't answer my question," said Victoria. "If they choose to declare war, will you adhere to their decision?" The stillness lingered as her father lay in his bed.

"I made a promise to resolve this conflict peacefully. I still intend to uphold it, for the realm and Gwen's safety." He handed his plate to her. Half of the fish and barely any of the vegetables had been eaten. "Now, go. I wish to rest."

She took the plate, hopping off the bed and leaving his chambers. It pained her to see her father so fragile. Even if he did contest Parliament's decision, there was little he could do to stop them. He no longer possessed the strength of will or spirit. Returning to the kitchen, she placed her father's leftovers on the floor for Artemis to feast on. She then made her way back to her chambers, climbing the series of stairs. Her eyes welled with tears as reality dawned on her. Her world as she knew it was unraveling. Her father's mortality was ever more present, her sister was still lost and possibly would remain so, and the war had a chance of reigniting. It all scared her, and in Gwen's absence, the responsibility of solving these issues fell onto her upon her father's death. She collapsed, curling up on one of the steps as the tears rolled down her cheeks. She sobbed relentlessly, broken and afraid.

26

The mesa which Danforth sat atop overlooked the rest of the valley like a fortress of eroded limestone. Little could be seen of the city from below, except for a handful of towers piercing the blue sky like needles. A steep, winding road wrapped itself around the stone cliff leading up to the city. The path was wide enough for horses to traverse, but in the chariot, there was a considerable risk of falling to certain death. An army stood no chance of making the climb for an assault. It's what made Danforth an impenetrable city second only to the capital and its wall. Damian, however, directed them away from the intended path, guiding them along the mesa's base. He motioned for Anden to slow the chariot near a strange formation of rocks with a crevice just large enough for a person to fit through.

"After all these years, I hope it hasn't caved in," said Damian hopping out of his seat.

They each squeezed through the opening, crawling on their hands and knees into a cavernous tunnel. Water trickled down the walls, and the pitter-patter of their feet splashing with each step echoed throughout the corridor. Damian led the way, holding a makeshift torch he crafted from a piece of dried wood and Wesley's used bandages soaked in gasoline. The rancid odor of feces grew more prevalent the deeper they traveled.

Gwen held a hand over her nose. "What is that putrid stench?"

"The sewer system runs through a few of the caverns," Damian explained. "This particular one might have been used as an escape tunnel in case of cave-ins."

More water, discolored and contaminated with filth, flooded the cavern reaching up to their ankles.

"Fucking hell," cursed Anden as he lifted his sandaled feet covered in waste.

A small waterfall poured from a stone cylinder jutting out of the rock. Gwen pinched her nose shut, but even that wasn't enough to keep the foul stench from reaching her nostrils. She gagged on the verge of vomiting. Once she was able to compose herself, Damian hoisted her up to a narrow walkway along the stream of sewage.

"How did you discover this cavern?" Gwen asked. "Something that practically serves as a backdoor into Danforth would be worth protecting."

"I agree," said Damian. "Although, I only happened to find it through luck. After escaping my execution, I fled into the sewer system, figuring the sewage had to go somewhere. It, of course, led to that cavern we came through only after stumbling in the dark for Emperor knows how long."

The sewage tunnel inclined slightly as they continued walking. The singular stream soon branched out into a mazelike series of tunnels. Along one of the walls was a ladder of metal rods. Before any of them climbed up, Anden shoved his hat onto Damian's head.

"Keep this on and your head down while we're in public," he said. "Don't need anyone recognizing you."

It occurred to Gwen she had never really seen Anden without his hat. Underneath was a flattened tuft of dark, brown hair, and his face held a youthful appearance. It didn't match his melancholy attitude at all. With Damian somewhat disguised, they climbed the ladder and exited the sewers through a brick archway. None of the citizens passing by on the cobblestone road noticed them crawl out of the hole. Their bodies were powdered with dirt, and sewage dripped from their boots. Anden pulled down a nearby poster and wiped the waste from his feet.

"Where to?" asked Wesley taking in the city with curious eyes.

"We can try hiding out at my old place," said Damian. "If they haven't burned it down."

They headed down the cobblestone road, Damian keeping his head tilted down so the hat covered most of his face. Militia soldiers, both graduated and recruits in training, meandered about, mingling with pedestrians. Royal blue banners affixed with the image of a white phoenix hung from various banisters along the streets. The wooden architecture reminded Gwen of the capital's northwest district, except many of the buildings possessed foundations built from stone. Wanted posters littered their walls, including a tattered one with a hand-drawn image of Damian. Another was plastered with the depiction of a hooded individual decorated in daggers and various other blades. Chills slithered down her spine, coursing throughout her body as she recognized Vargo Vasallo, the assassin who made an attempt on her father's life.

Anden noticed her visible discomfort and followed her gaze to the poster, narrowing his eyes. They continued following Damian and Wesley, reaching a bustling plaza square where a troupe of musicians performed in front of an exquisite, decorative fountain. Down a long street piercing the center of the square and filled with merchants of every kind stood the guildhall, a commanding tower at the epicenter of the city. It served as a residence for the high-ranking officials, including Noreen. At the edge of the plaza, among a cluster of other buildings, rested a rundown house. The door hung by a single hinge, and the windows on the lower floor were shattered.

"Best to go around the back, so no one grows suspicious," Damian suggested.

They followed him into an alley toward the back of the house. Here, there was no door, only an opening in the wall. Inside, cobwebs decorated the doorframes and the railing along the stairway. A thick layer of dust and dirt coated the floorboards. Furniture was strewn about in every room. Wesley sauntered into the kitchen, where the cabinets were open, revealing sets of dusty bowls, plates, pots, pans, and silverware. The pantry was empty, and what little food remained was long soiled.

Damian removed the hat from his head and returned it to Anden. "We can stay here while we formulate a plan to get Lady Gwen to Ambassador Archer."

"Plan?" Anden scoffed. "She's the princess. She can just walk through the front door."

"Under normal circumstances, but the strange behavior you mentioned about the soldiers in Lundur makes me think otherwise. We need to be cautious. If the ambassador is the only one she trusts, then that's who needs to find her first."

Anden sat on one of the lower steps on the staircase. "Oh, that'll be easy. Why don't we just go knock on her front door? Send an anonymous note? *'Hey, heard you were looking for the princess. You can find her here.'"*

Wesley emerged from the kitchen doorway. "That's not a bad idea. Obviously, the wording could use work, but pique her interest with something. Lure her out of her tower to find Gwen. We watch from a distance to make sure it goes down smoothly."

Damian crossed his arms in annoyance. "If she doesn't decide to send soldiers or her Militia captain to handle it."

"Who I heard during my time in Sandur is now your former vice-captain, Edward," said Wesley. "He was an astute and noble lad. I doubt he'd be corrupt in any way to harm the princess."

Gwen didn't like being talked about like she wasn't present in the room. "Excuse me, but since my life might be on the line, shouldn't I have a say in things?"

The three men looked at each other in silence before turning to her.

"Firstly," she said, "if we're going to discuss this, it should be over some dinner." Hunger ate at her stomach, and she longed for a nice homecooked meal after days of traveling.

"Here, here," cheered Wesley. "Use some of that coin we earned to pick up some fresh ingredients for a proper meal. That food back at the outpost was a bit tough and bland."

"If you're going to peruse the market, then I'll run an errand as well," said Anden, rising from the stairs.

"Fine," said Damian. "We'll discuss the matter further after eating." He marched up the stairs, pushing past Anden.

Gwen entered the kitchen and, upon seeing all the dirty dishes, started to fill the sink with water. It felt good to return to a familiar form of society. For days, they journeyed across the eastern part of the continent, avoiding all kinds of dangers. While a part of her still did not wish to return home, having not yet seen the rest of the kingdom, she was able to visit a few of the towns and cities. She got to see the beautiful northern forests and bear witness to the Core outpost hidden there, as well as survive a daunting trek through the ghost town of Kelveux. She also learned that the truce had not been upheld, along with a possible coup within the Militia. Though her journey had been cut short, she learned much about the outside world and what changes needed considering.

27

Anden moseyed across the plaza under the ever-watchful gaze of Cain Bezok's statue atop the fountain. He always hated that piece of carved stone, even as a kid. Amid the citizens meandering about completing their errands and Militia recruits loitering during their free time, its cold eyes always seemed to find him. Markets lined the strip connecting the plaza to the guildhall, but Anden had no interest in perusing their shelves. The spirit he required could not be found in any shop. Escaping into an alley, he snaked his way through the network of buildings and braced himself to traverse old memories he held dear.

Following a main road, he reached a familiar part of the city constructed of brick and stone surrounded by acres of open land. Rows of barracks stretched out across the area with a modest bell tower standing at the helm. The bell's bronze color had long been rusted over from years, maybe even centuries, of exposure to the elements. The earthy smell saturated his nose and triggered memories of his youth to flash in his mind. The endless days of sparring and acquiring a collection of bruises along with serene meditation and the rowdy nights of drunken revelry. A smile crossed his face. His eyes scanned the buildings for a specific window. It was the fifth window from the right on the seventh floor of the fourth barrack. Gazing at it, he wondered which unfortunate soul currently resided there and if their experience differed from his in any way.

Approaching the bell tower, Anden stood before a metal grate buried into the ground. Underneath the Militia training grounds existed a network of tunnels supposedly dating back to when Danforth was first founded. Nowadays, they have been converted into bunkers for citizens to hide in case of an attack. Since the odds of that were unlikely, the tunnels had gone unused for decades. He bent over and stuck his fingers between the grating, swinging it open like a trap door. Jumping down, he entered a dark cavern that stretched into further darkness both in front and behind him. Just a few paces away, directly under where the bell tower stood, was a busted, wooden crate covered by a worn sheet of cloth. He peeled it back to unveil a collection of half-empty bottles containing an array of liquors. Sifting through them, he found one with the seal unbroken. It was an old Bushgrove whiskey he obtained before graduating from a recruit into a full-fledged soldier of the Militia but never found the opportunity to open it. It weighed heavy in his hand, being a prized possession back in a time when donning the phoenix on his back gave him pride.

He climbed out of the tunnel and shut the grate behind him. The sun settled on the horizon as he journeyed back to the plaza. The return trip seemed faster as he found himself amid the bustling crowds near the strip. Snaking through the alleys again, he heard harsh whispers reverberate off the walls. Following the sounds, he peered around a corner and in a narrow alley were two men adorned in blue padded jackets. One of them was an intellectual-looking man with brass hair, a drooping nose, and full-moon spectacles. Anden recognized him as Edward Quinn, who replaced Damian as captain of the Third Division. With him was Ben Green in the middle of a lecture.

"This peace is nothing more than a façade," said Ben. "Rahm only needs one more guaranteed vote for a majority."

"I'm sorry, Captain," said Edward, "but Ambassador Archer is not an impulsive individual. She'll weigh the options and possible consequences before reaching a decision."

Ben grew frustrated. "Then persuade her. You're the ranking officer in this division, and this is a military matter. Your word must hold some weight."

"I cannot force her even if I wanted to. Besides, she's a bright woman, and I trust her judgment, whatever it may be. We'll just have to wait and see what the conclave will hold."

"Bright." Ben shook his head, pacing. "She has no allies in Parliament. Not sure I would call someone like that bright. Although, swaying the vote in Rahm's favor could change that. His allies would become hers."

"You think she cares about having allies in Parliament?" Edward scoffed. "You don't know the ambassador very well. She only cares about her duty to the kingdom and doesn't give a damn for what you or I or even the chancellor could think of her."

"I hope she contemplates the consequences that while they waste time bickering in a stone prison, the rebels will be making their move. Her inability to act and, by extension yours, may cost hundreds or even thousands of lives. I would consider if you could bear that weight on your soul." Ben stomped out of the alley, leaving Edward to contemplate his words.

Anden remained hidden behind the corner as Edward stood there for a moment in silence. After he finally left, Anden dashed through the rest of the alleys and out to the plaza. He cared little for politics, but a conclave being called meant Noreen wouldn't remain in Danforth for much longer. If they were to ensure Gwen's safe return to the capital, it would have to be now.

28

Gwen wiped the final plate dry and set it on the counter with the others. Exhausted, she slumped into a nearby chair, tossing the rag over her shoulder. Everything was now prepared for Wesley's return to cook them a bountiful meal. Damian remained quiet the entire time, never venturing downstairs. Figuring she should check on him, Gwen filled a tankard with water and carried it upstairs. Damian brooded in the corner of what she assumed to be his bedroom, sharpening his sword. The bed was overturned, and the vanity gutted, leaving clothes cluttered on the floor. He halted his blade on the whetstone upon noticing her enter.

"Something wrong?" he asked in a gentle voice.

Gwen placed the tankard on the table where he toiled. "I brought you some water."

"Thank you." He lifted the tankard and took a sip. Setting it aside, he continued sharpening. The blade hissed as its edge dragged across the block. Gwen watched for a few silent moments before turning to leave. "Do you fear me, my lady?"

"I'm not sure," she said. "Shocked more than anything. Speaking true, I wasn't sure if we found you that you wouldn't just kill us. The stories paint you as a monster, but you seem to be a man of honor."

"Men can be as fierce as the wildest fleshlings," said Damian. "Just because they have a human face doesn't mean they are one."

"So, are you a monster? Did you kill your own men in cold blood as the stories say?"

Damian placed his sword on the table and turned to face her. His gray eyes stared at her intently as he rested his chin on his hands. "There was a nobleman, one of the people responsible for giving us this." He pulled out a clear vial filled with gasoline. "He was traveling back to the Island of Tears, and because of the war, he required an escort. A small group of men and I were tasked with protecting him from Laminfell to a small village north of White Horn, where Balavan would accompany him for the rest of the trip. We crossed the border into the fourth division without any trouble, arriving the night before the transfer. We lodged at an inn to wait and rest."

His gaze darkened with sorrow as he paused for a moment.

"That night, I experienced dreams and nightmares unlike any other. I remember hearing whispers soothing my mind into some sort of compliance. It felt like I was being restrained, bound by something I couldn't see. I fought against the restraints, and the whispers turned into screams. The words dug into me like thorns against my flesh. I awoke to see a shadowy figure looming over me brandishing a dagger. I was able to catch the blade and fight him off. I reached for my sword."

Grabbing the blade from the table, he jabbed it into the floor as if reenacting the scene.

"I pierced my blade through his chest. It was only then that I realized it was one of my own men. Others dashed into the room to see me draw the sword from his corpse. I tried to explain myself, but they all rushed me with the intent to kill. I cut them down in what I thought was self-defense. The commotion caused people to rush out of the inn, including the nobleman. The following morning, Balavan and his men arrived already having heard what happened. I turned myself in and went to trial. I was convicted of treachery and sentenced to death. To this day, I don't know if something was wrong with my men or me."

He gazed at his reflection in the blade, lost in grief. Gwen managed to sit on the edge of the bedframe across from him. She wrapped a hand around the hilt of the sword and set it aside so he could focus on her sympathetic stare.

"When I return to the palace, it won't be too much longer before I'm crowned queen," she said. "I'll have the power to at least pardon you of the crime. Think of it as repayment for helping me."

He averted his eyes, shaking his head. "Parliament would never agree to it. Besides, I've been perceived as a monster for five years now. That won't change because you say so."

The thud of the front door opening interrupted their conversation. Damian stood from his seat and grabbed his sword from the wall, sheathing it behind his back. "At least one of them seems to have returned. We should go see if they need any help."

Gwen stayed in the messy room a moment longer. Perhaps he was going mad, hearing whispers in his sleep, but the grief-stricken look upon his hardened face told her he was ashamed. He wasn't the monster she'd overheard soldiers speak of. He possessed a conscience, one that burdened him with his mistakes. Rising to her feet, she followed Damian downstairs. Vegetables and meat spilled onto the kitchen table from a burlap sack. Wesley flew around, prepping utensils for cooking. His erratic movements reminded her of the cooks assisting Helmond back at the palace. Damian leaned against the wall chewing on a carrot he took from the sack. As Gwen entered, Wesley shot her a wide grin.

"I can't believe you cleaned all of them," he said. "I can immediately start cooking. Hopefully, it shouldn't take too long. Damian, is there any wood we can burn for the oven?"

"I'm sure we can scrounge some up," Damian said, "but keep the flames low. Don't want to attract any attention that someone's here."

"Of course. Of course."

Damian left the kitchen for a few minutes and returned with splintered wood, probably from some part of the house that was damaged. Stacking them into the oven, he poured a small amount of gasoline over the wood before setting it ablaze.

Evening befell nightfall as Wesley pulled out a thick piece of roasted ham. Slamming it onto the counter, he brandished a knife and started slicing it into thin pieces. The front door barged open, and Anden came racing in holding a large bottle filled with an auburn liquid.

"Just in time," said Wesley. "Meat just came out of the oven. We'll be able to eat after I cut some slices."

Anden glanced about with a panicked expression catching his breath.

"What's wrong?" asked Gwen.

"We may have a problem," he said. "Green is in the city, and I overheard him talking to Edward about an upcoming conclave. He was trying to get him to persuade Noreen into siding with Rahm on the vote."

"Rahm must be desperate," added Damian, pinching his hairless chin. "Usually, it's easier to buy out Weyman. Regardless, we're short on time. If a conclave has been called, Noreen will be leaving for the capital soon."

"My thoughts exactly," agreed Anden.

"Can we continue this discussion while eating?" said Wesley filling plates with steaming hot food. "I didn't buy these ingredients and spend time cooking just for it to go cold."

Thunder erupted, shaking the entire house, followed by a frenzied commotion from outside. The four of them raced to the windows to see flashes light up the sky and flames spread in the distance. People sprinted across the plaza, screaming as hellfire rained from above. Another eruption of thunder shook the house. Anden ripped open the front door to get a better look at the scene. Gwen's mouth fell agape in horror. Hovering over them, over the city of Danforth, was a fortress of some kind. Anden and Damian were just as speechless.

The only one to have anything to say was Wesley. "Looks like dinner is going to waste after all."

29

Plumes of smoke glowed a reddish hue as if the sun had never set. The sight reminded Reed of that night on the boat when she watched the village burn. The night when her uncle and mother died. The cannon fire sang a symphonic tune as she watched chaos consume the city from the helm of Watts' machine. Long had she waited for this moment when they could deal a devastating blow to the kingdom.

Vargo strutted across the bridge with a nasty cackle. "Fantastic. An entire city burning at your feet. That boy of yours is a true master of his craft. It almost seems like you don't need me at all."

"Your time will come soon enough," said Reed. "If not here, then at the capital."

That rotten smile of yellow teeth peeked out from his hood. "A rematch with Gunnway is satisfactory enough. I'd also ask to slit the old man's throat, but I'm guessing you want that luxury for yourself. 'Blood nourishing the ashes' and all that nonsense. I will request the other daughter, though."

"It's too early to talk about taking the capital," said Elliot. "We still have Danforth to conquer and a Militia to weaken."

Reed rounded on her high overseer, her eyes ablaze with fury. "I don't need lecturing on what must be done. I've prepared for this moment since childhood and dreamed of it every night I rested my head. I was born for this."

Elliot respectfully backed off, and Vargo continued to stare at the fiery haze below. Reed directed her attention to the guildhall towering above the other buildings. Its peak reached high enough to scrape the ship's lower decks, and the reflection of dancing flames shimmered in its windows. The structure became a sore to her eyes.

"General Watts," she called out.

The eager young man appeared before her, snapping to attention.

"I want that structure turned to rubble."

Nodding his head, the engineer relayed the orders into a metallic cone that carried his voice through a series of metal veins across the entire ship. They glided through the sky, positioning themselves in front of the tower. With a single command, a volley of cannon fire was unleashed, crumbling the stone until it collapsed. A cloud of debris, dust, and soot blanketed the surrounding area as a pile of rubble stood in place of the guildhall. Cheers erupted throughout the bridge, but Reed remained stoic.

"Send out troops to raid the city," she commanded Elliot.

Her high overseer excused himself from the bridge to rally troops. Cannon fire was a useful enough tool, but she was aware of the underground bunkers. To keep them from hiding there, it required the traditional approach of a raid utilizing soldiers.

"Shall I join in the fun?" asked Vargo.

"Stay here for the time being," said Reed. "If the captain becomes a problem, then you have my permission to kill him."

The assassin tapped a thin, bony finger to his chin. "Remind me again, who captains this division?"

"Edward Quinn, former vice-captain under the Burnt Coat."

"I hope he proves just as ruthless as his former senior officer," Vargo said with a sneer. "Otherwise, killing him might turn out to be disappointing."

Reed didn't care whether Vargo found pleasure in the work or not as long as it got done. She laid her eyes on the inferno below once more. She could feel the fires' heat on her skin; they burned so hot. The phoenix would not rise from these ashes. From the kingdom's remains, those who have suffered would emerge, their shackles broken, to live a life of true freedom.

30

Sparks and embers floated through the air like glowing flakes of snow. Terrified shrieks drowned out the thundering sound of the fortress's artillery above. A thick haze of smoke blanketed the square as Anden and the others stood awestruck as the guildhall collapsed. Gwen sank to her knees in despair while Damian gripped the hilt of his sword, ready to draw. Anden grabbed Gwen's wrist, pulling her to her feet.

"Come on," he said. "We need to get out of here."

Damian glared at Anden. "You can't expect us to leave the city to burn."

"Why not? What do you expect us to do? Fight? Please, explain how we are to fight that." He pointed a finger at the aircraft obscuring the sky.

"I'm not sure," Damian admitted, "but when has that ever stopped us before?"

"This is beyond us. This is a war. A war we have no part in."

"Yes, we do." Damian's eyes glided over to Gwen, trembling as a panicked crowd swarmed them. "You think the rebels will stop here? They'll rain down a fire stretching all the way to the capital. If we're to make sure the princess returns home, then we need to make sure she has a home to return to."

Wesley tugged on Anden's shoulder. "You helped put an end to the rebellion's grasp on Sandur. Why should this be any different?"

"Because I care about you," said Anden. "Both of you. I don't give a shit about this city or its people. We had a plan, and now it's ruined. The best thing we can do right now is escape and figure something else out."

Damian stared at him with his stoic expression. It never angered Anden as much as it did now. "If you want to leave, then leave. Meanwhile, I'm going to do what I can for these people." Turning, he started to walk away from them.

Anden tore at Damian's shoulder, spinning him around. "Has it been your goal these past few years to die in some altruistic manner? You still can't get over the fact that we saved you from death. We did, okay? What happened, happened. You're here, and you're alive, so cherish it rather than throw it away."

"You don't understand," said Damian. "Just because you saved me, it didn't erase my guilt, so I sought redemption for my mistake. By joining the Core, I hoped to serve the continent in a different way, still upholding a duty to protect the people of this kingdom. That's why I can't walk away from this."

Anden clenched his jaw. He had no desire for redemption or to be a hero. He had no interest in the war between the kingdom and the rebellion. For the past five long years, all he ever wanted was this—being reunited with his friends. Ones he originally swore never to see again. Now that they were together, he was afraid to lose them.

Gwen grabbed hold of his arm and stared at him with her large, hazel eyes. In the light of the surrounding fires, they burned into him. "If there is something you can do, please do it. These people and everyone else throughout the kingdom don't deserve this."

She didn't know it, but Anden owed her more than the silver she paid. If it wasn't for their chance encounter, he would never have had the opportunity to reunite with his friends.

Reaching into his pockets, he pulled out the ring of keys and placed them in her hand. "You know where the chariot is. Take the sewage tunnels back to the cavern and wait for us there. If we don't come back… You'll just have to cross that bridge when you get there."

She placed her other hand over his. "None of you can die until you get me home." She glanced around at the three of them. "You hear me? None of you get to die yet. That's an order."

They each looked back at her with intense gazes as gunshots erupted amidst the crowd. Rebel forces stormed the streets, terrorizing the fleeing mob.

"Go," barked Anden.

Gwen took off, disappearing in a swarm of citizens.

They drew their weapons, Wesley his pistols, Damian his bastard sword, and Anden his three-sectioned staff. Damian led the charge, dodging gunfire and barreling through the rebel troops with swings of his sword like a gardener hacking weeds. Anden provided support, taking a wide sweep for a flanking position, and attacked the swordsmen, who shifted their focus to Damian. He twirled the ends of his weapon, unleashing a flurry of blows that sent bodies collapsing to the ground. Wesley kept a distance, returning a hail of gunfire to the rebel marksmen aiming down their rifles. The platoon's numbers dwindled until only the three of them remained standing. Blood dripped off the metal from Anden and Damian's weapons. Wesley rolled one of the bodies over with his foot, scowling at the red band wrapped around their arm.

Damian scanned the surrounding area. "If they're coming from that thing in the sky, they must be landing somewhere."

Wesley turned his sharp eyes upward, squinting. "This way."

They stepped over the fresh corpses following him into the merchant strip. Debris from the buildings cluttered the road, and store owners tried to salvage whatever merchandise they could. One of them, a stout, older gentleman, watched his store burn with glassy eyes. He reminded Anden of Eli in a way, and as they passed by, the man didn't move.

Reaching the ruins of the guildhall at the end of the road, a small platoon of rebels floated down, touching their boots to the ground. Their hands fumbled at their waists, untethering a rope of some kind. Anden, Damian, and Wesley ambushed the group, slaughtering them. Many weren't even able to draw their swords before being killed. Ropes dangled around them in the aftermath, and Anden investigated one of them. The fibers pricked his fingers as he touched it. The material wasn't hemp, but something tougher with a metallic chill.

"Hope you're not afraid of heights," Wesley quipped as he started to climb one of the other ropes.

Damian followed suit. Grabbing hold, Anden began climbing as well. His hands found it challenging to maintain a proper grip. After climbing a few feet, they each shot upward, the rope ascending toward the fortress of its own volition. Higher and higher they went. Anden could see the edge of the mesa and a bird's perspective of Danforth burning. There was scarcely a section of the city that hadn't gone up in flames. The

227

wind was vicious at such a height, beating the clothes off their backs. Anden held his hat firm to his head as they careened toward a metal platform jutting out from the side of the structure.

Anden hoisted himself onto the platform, coming face to face with a shocked rebel. Seizing the man's jacket, Anden flung him over the edge, his scream fading as he fell. Damian and Wesley climbed onto the other platforms interconnected by a single grate walkway, where they reconvened. The hum of the fortress and howling wind overpowered their voices, effectively rendering them mute. Two riflemen standing on the opposite end of the walkway fired an onslaught of bullets, forcing them to take cover. Wesley returned fire, allowing them to cross the walkway to a metal door affixed with a similar contraption to the one in Kelveux. Damian twisted the wheel and turned the mechanisms that opened the door, revealing a labyrinth constructed of metal walls and pipes.

Overhead, a web of steel beams wove together into a dome-shaped structure covered by a large fabric. They wandered through a few corridors before running into a woman covered in grease and sporting a thick pair of goggles. Seeing them, she froze for a moment before fleeing. Anden gave chase, navigating the halls by following the sound of her boots pounding against the metal floor.

When he caught up to her, she was screaming into a strange cone. "Intruders in sector eight, lower floor. I repeat, intruders in sector eight, lower—"

Anden threw a hand over her mouth and restrained her against the wall. She continued screaming muffled words into his hand. It took a sharp twist of her arm to silence her.

"I'm going to remove my hand," he said as Damian and Wesley rounded the corner. "When I do, you're going to tell us what this thing is and how to shut it down." He gave her a stern look before removing his hand.

"I'm not telling you anything," she spat. "You Militia lap dogs."

Wesley cocked his pistol, pressing the barrel into her temple. "We're not with the Militia, and unless you want a bullet ripping through your skull, you better talk."

She glared at them in a rage, breathing heavily. "You'll want the bridge. It controls the ship and is located at the front."

Wesley lowered his gun.

"Take us there," demanded Anden, but as he moved to pull her from the wall, a dagger pierced her face. Her limp body slid out of Anden's grasp and onto the floor. From one of the hallways emerged a hooded figure armed with various types of blades that were displayed across his chest and hips. White eyes peered at them from behind the hood, landing on Damian.

"How exciting," he said. "I was expecting to find nothing but a few stowaway rats needing extermination. Imagine my surprise to see the Burnt Coat standing before me. This night certainly holds its fair share of startling developments." His foggy gaze lingered on Wesley and Anden. "If you two are here, I assume the girl is as well."

They exchanged a worried glance before narrowing their eyes back at the man.

"We don't know what you're talking about," said Wesley.

The hooded man snickered. "No need to play dumb. I know she was with you in Nabal."

"What interest is she to you?" asked Anden with gritted teeth.

"Personally, none. Although, I do have a client who requires a member of the royal bloodline. I'd hoped to deliver them the king, but that didn't quite work out."

Anden realized who it was confronting them. He remembered the wanted poster that unsettled Gwen when they entered the city. A hooded individual decorated in steel with piercing, white eyes. Vargo Vasallo.

"If the girl is here," he continued, "I can't afford to miss this opportunity. I do have a debt to repay." He lowered his hood to reveal the grotesque, decomposed flesh of his face. The musculature of his jaw was exposed, the lids of his eyes were missing, and his nose was replaced by a gaping hole. Small patches of hair stuck out of his mostly bald and veiny head. A fleshling looked more alive. He unsheathed a sword from his hip, the steel singing a dreary tune.

"He can't take all three of us," said Wesley.

"No," said Damian, his sword already drawn. "The longer this thing remains in the sky, the more the city will burn, and more people will die. You and Anden search for the bridge. I'll hold off the assassin."

Anden lowered his voice so Vargo couldn't hear. "You might be able to take him alone at your best, but you're still hindered by your injury. It's not like I want to fight the guy, but I have the best chance of holding him off alone."

Damian raised his blade, blocking Anden and Wesley from Vargo. "I'm a member of the Hunters' Core. It's my duty to cleanse the continent of every vile creature and dark spawn we find. This thing standing before us is a monster wearing human flesh."

"You're right," the assassin hissed. "I'm no longer human, but above it. I've surpassed even the broken limits of your old tradition. I proved it against Gunnway, and I'll do it again with you."

"Go," Damian demanded.

Reluctantly, Anden and Wesley left Damian alone with Vargo, winding through the metal corridors with no idea whether it was the right path or not. Behind them echoed the clashing of swords and Vargo's chilling laughter.

31

Chaos spread throughout the city, and Gwen found herself in the midst of it all. One amongst the herd stampeding through the streets to seek safety. Fire continued to rain down, setting the buildings ablaze and casting a fog of black smoke that suffocated her lungs. She searched for a sewage drain to hide in and wait for the assault to cease, but rampant citizens crowded her vision. They shoved her around until she collapsed and the people behind her kicked and trampled her body. Blessed with a reprieve, Gwen scurried off the cobblestone road to a nearby wall. Her body ached as she caught her breath. Tears streamed down her face, but she couldn't stop them. Everything was in disarray and madness. The flames would burn the city until all that remained was a graveyard of cinders and ash littered with the corpses of its people. She would most likely be one of them. She wasn't a warrior like her sister or father. Instead of training with a sword, she studied with books. War wasn't a foreign concept, not in the least. She knew the consequences of wars, the outcomes, and history, but she never learned how to fight in one.

An abandoned child teetered across the street, crying. No one seemed to notice the young boy wailing for help, calling for his mother. Gwen touched the hilt of the short sword strapped to her side. Wiping the tears from her cheek, she rose to her feet and sprinted toward the boy. Scooping him up in a warm embrace, she patted his head in comfort.

"It's okay," she assured. "It's going to be okay."

A Militia soldier appeared, urging her forward.

"Come with me, miss," he said. "You and the child will be safe in the underground bunkers."

Gwen followed the soldier, clutching the boy tightly to her body. They picked up two others along the way, a man and a middle-aged woman. Together, their small group waded through the destruction, desperate to reach the bunkers. Gunfire whizzed by, forcing them to take cover.

"Damn rebels," grumbled the soldier, loading a shot into his pistol. Peeking around the corner, he fired, unleashing a flash of white smoke. He nodded them down the alleyway. "We'll go around and hopefully avoid more gunfire."

As they ventured through the alley, the sound of gunshots sent the child into a fit of crying. Gwen tried to calm him, but it was no use.

"Dreadful," said the middle-aged woman. "I thought there

was a truce between the kingdom and the rebellion."

"Obviously, the rebels changed their mind," said the man.

Rounding a corner, the soldier motioned for them to lay low while he scouted the area ahead. "The coast is clear."

They all took off from the alley back onto the main road. In the distance, an open field laid with rows of buildings silhouetted in the glow of the flames. The Militia soldier informed them they were nearing the bunkers when, suddenly, they were ambushed by a group of rebels. Gwen and the middle-aged woman fled to hide. The man and the soldier engaged the rebels in combat. The soldier drew his sword and cut one of them down, locking blades with another. The man grappled with the third rebel for his sword. Gwen and the woman hid behind an empty carriage as everything unfolded. They watched as the rebel punched the man, pulling his blade free and stabbing him through the chest. The soldier parried a strike and slashed the other rebel's neck open. The last rebel withdrew his sword from the man's body and charged the soldier, knocking him to the ground. The two men dropped their weapons and started pummeling each other with their fists.

"We should go," whimpered the woman. "He said the bunkers weren't far."

Gwen ignored her and instead thrust the young boy into her arms. Drawing the short sword, she dashed at the two men. The rebel cradled the soldier, pinning him to the ground as his fists continued to fly. Gwen held the sword in front of her as she neared them and rammed it forward, piercing the rebel's back. Its sharp edge cut through him like a steak knife through a tender piece of meat. Blood dripped onto the soldier as the rebel fell onto his side, dead.

As his corpse slid off the blade, Gwen stared at the crimson trails streaking across its steel. The dead rebel stared at her with blank, lifeless eyes as blood spilled from his mouth. Her heart quivered. She couldn't believe she actually killed someone. The act itself was so easy, requiring no thought. She did it without almost realizing it. Was taking a life really so easy? The sword trembled in her hands as her breathing drowned out the surrounding chaos.

The soldier rose and retrieved his sword. Blood ran down his nose, and his right eye started to swell. "Thank you," he said. "I might owe you my life." Noticing her shock, he touched a hand to her shoulder. "Are you okay?"

Gwen couldn't take it anymore. Bending over, she spewed a mouthful of vomit.

"It's okay," assured the soldier. "Never had to kill anyone, have you? It can be tough, but you need to get to the bunkers."

The middle-aged woman hurried over to them, holding the boy. Sheathing her sword, Gwen wiped an arm over her mouth and turned to the woman. "Take care of him. Make sure to find someone who will give him a home."

Without another word, she sprinted down the street in the opposite direction of the bunkers. The soldier called after her, but she didn't stop. She couldn't stop. She needed to find Damian, needed to find Wesley, and needed to find Anden. She wasn't sure about the outcome of this battle or if the Militia would emerge victorious. All she wanted at that moment was to find her companions. She wanted to tell Anden that he was right about the rest of the continent. He was always right. The world really was nothing but a shithole.

32

Searching for the bridge was as tough as digging through a noblewoman's dress for her knickers. Every corridor they entered seemed identical to the last to the point Anden believed they were going in circles. A handful of rebels crossed their path, but they were a minor inconvenience. After dealing with them, Anden and Wesley paused for a moment to collect their thoughts.

"We're not getting anywhere like this," said Anden. Wesley noticed an upper level of rafters above them. "Help me get up there," he said. "I might be able to see the bridge and help guide you there." He lured Anden to a nearby wall just beneath the rafters.

Anden linked his hands together and lowered into a squat. Wesley sprinted toward him, placing a foot into Anden's hands as he catapulted him up. Wesley managed to grab the edge by his fingertips and hoisted himself onto the rafter, surveying the area.

"I think I see it," he called down. "Turn back and take the first left you can. I'll meet you over there."

Turning on his heels, Anden backtracked through the hall, taking the first left he came across. From there, Wesley shouted down directions as they navigated the maze. Rebels tried stopping them, but they were a one-man army on two fronts. Before long, they entered a spacious room overlooked by a wall of glass. On the other side, people were gathered around strange devices with levers, buttons, and pullies.

Wesley jumped down from the rafters. "That looks like the control center of this thing."

"Then let's bring it down," said Anden.

A giant door slammed shut behind them, blocking the exit. They rushed for the doorway on the opposite end of the room, but it was sealed shut as well. The disembodied voice of a woman filled the room.

"Not only have you boarded our ship, but you've also somehow evaded Vargo's clutches. Saying I'm impressed would be an understatement." Reed Skokna stood on the other side of the glass, speaking into one of those strange metal cones. "You don't wear the colors or crest of the Militia. If you're mercenaries of some kind, I'm sure we can come to a more than beneficial agreement for you."

Wesley drew his pistol and fired three shots into the glass. It cracked but did not break. He fired three more, yielding the same result.

"You'll need a bit more than that to break this glass," she said.

"That's why I carry a second pistol." Wesley's hand moved for his other gun, but before drawing it, the floor at the center of the room dropped open.

A surge of wind sucked them toward the gaping chasm. Anden grabbed a nearby railing, flinging out his three-section staff for Wesley. He managed to grab the last rod in the link as he skidded along the floor. Anden strained to pull them both closer to the railing, but pulling a grown man against a gale-force wind was nearly impossible. Being tossed about, Wesley fumbled for his other pistol, reaching across his body into the opposite holster. Fishing it out, he steadied his aim and unloaded six shots. The bullets cracked the glass snow white, with the sixth shattering it completely. A few people were flung from the bridge into the massive hole. Anden's grip loosened around the railing as his strength started to fail him. His fingers uncurled from the bar, slipping and sending them hurtling through the air with no hope of stopping. Reaching the edge of the hole, the floor sealed itself back up as the two men jostled around on the floor.

Picking himself up, Anden converted his three-section staff into one and used it to vault up to the broken pane of glass. The bridge was in disarray, with people fleeing the room after the sudden breach. Reed swiped at him with twin daggers. Her strikes were quick and precise. Anden twirled his staff around his body to keep her at a distance. She stayed at the edge of his reach, waiting for the opportune moment to strike when his guard faltered. That moment came as a bullet grazed his arm, causing him to drop his staff. Smoke drifted from the barrel of a pistol held by a man whose face folded over itself in wrinkles. The woman thrust both daggers forward, and Anden grabbed her wrists, the tips of the blades pricking his skin. The weight of her strength pressed into him, trying to sink them deeper. With a bit more leverage, she could probably do it. Restrained, she delivered a sharp knee to his groin, weakening Anden's legs. Having partaken in many barfights, Anden swallowed the pain, proving resilient. Twisting her arms, the daggers fell from her grasp. Anden shifted his body weight and tackled her to the ground. As he did so, the butt of the wrinkled man's pistol knocked him aside. Anden dove for his staff, swept the man's feet from under him, and blocked another strike from Reed.

"Durham," she called out, grappling against Anden, "reload and shoot him."

The man fumbled for another bullet as the pistol flew out of his hand in a splatter of blood. He collapsed in a fit of pain, clutching his crimson-soaked hand that now only had three fingers. Wesley climbed up from the large room below, gun drawn. Reed disengaged and sprinted out a side door, escaping. Wesley moved to chase, but Anden stopped him.

"Leave her," he said. "We need to take this thing out of the sky."

Wesley picked the man writhing on the floor up by the collar of his jacket. "Tell us how to bring this thing down."

The man said nothing. Wesley dropped him back to the floor and fired a shot into his kneecap. He howled in pain.

"If you choose to stay silent, I've still got the other knee."

"No," the man pleaded. "The levers. Use the levers."

"Thank you." Wesley pistol-whipped him into unconsciousness before making his way to the levers. There were six in total, divided between two consoles, all in various positions.

"You think you can figure it out?" Anden asked.

"Probably," Wesley replied. "With some trial and error, of course."

"I'm going to help Damian. Hopefully, he's still alive."

As Wesley tinkered with the levers, Anden leaped down from the bridge back into the spacious room. The large door blocking their way disappeared, allowing him to cross the labyrinth of corridors. He raced through the winding hallways trying to remember their original route. Instinct guided him as his mind was too preoccupied with Damian's condition fighting such a skilled opponent. The fortress shifted, making him stumble into the walls, but he continued sprinting. He came to a halt upon hearing the sound of metal clinking. Strolling down the corridor was the decayed visage of Vargo, his sword dripping with blood.

"Good," he said. "You saved me the trouble of hunting you down."

Anden readied his staff, taking a wide stance. "Where's Damian?"

Even without lips, Anden could tell the assassin was smiling. "He wasn't useful to me. Wouldn't give up the princess's location. You might be able to offer a bit more than him."

Anden gritted his teeth. "You ain't getting shit out of me."

He pointed the edge of his blade at Anden. "We'll see."

Like a ghost, the assassin weightlessly drifted through the air. He was on Anden in a moment, overwhelming him. Anden checked as many strikes as he could with his staff, but Vargo was relentless. Some attacks passed through Anden's defenses, cutting his shoulder, thigh, then cheek. These weren't nicks either. The jagged edge of his blade cut deep. Fighting in a narrow corridor proved a disadvantage since his staff was better utilized for open areas. Twisting a mechanism in the middle rod, the chains unraveled into the three-section staff, and he whipped it around wildly. It caught Vargo off guard just enough for Anden to distance himself.

Anden caught his breath before the assassin closed in on him again. Charging forward, he seemed to pass through

Anden, flanking him from behind. Was it pure speed or something more? No time to think. The assassin thrust his blade, and Anden twisted a chain around the sword, halting it at his side. Slamming an elbow into the flat end of the steel, he broke it in half. Vargo snatched a dagger strapped to his body and swung upward. Anden tilted his head back, the edge cutting the brim of his bucket hat. Using half of the blade still intact, Vargo jabbed the broken steel into Anden's leg, followed by piercing the dagger into his shoulder. Anden's weapon fell from his grasp as he was forced into a wall.

"Now," hissed the assassin, "it's time to talk." His rotting face hovered close to Anden's. The stench of his breath wreaked more than Danforth's sewers. "Tell me, where is the princess?"

Anden groaned through the pain, "Fuck off."

"I know she's with you. Tell me, or I'll drag out your death until you're begging for it to end."

Anden spat at Vargo's face. The saliva trailed down what little flesh remained. The assassin twisted the blade in Anden's leg. The pain shot up his body like a bolt of lightning. He clenched his jaw so tight, the muscles in his neck strained.

Vargo kissed his rows of yellow teeth to Anden's ear. "I've seen many men like you. Abandoned by the world to suffer, and I have witnessed what lies beyond. Only more suffering. Giving up the girl will be the wisest thing you do. Her blood possesses the power to end it all. No more suffering."

Anden whispered back, "As I said before, fuck off."

Vargo withdrew himself from Anden's ear and proceeded to twist both the dagger and broken blade deeper into his flesh. Blood gushed out of the wounds dripping onto the floor and forming crimson puddles. As Vargo cackled at Anden's suffering, a shadow ambled up behind him. Its footsteps were masked by Anden's cries of pain. Lifting an arm, it lodged a sharp, black object into the assassin's neck. A fountain of dark blood spayed out as Vargo released Anden and stumbled, falling to the floor. Glancing up, Anden saw Damian leaning on the hilt of his sword like a crutch with his torso painted red.

"Are you okay?" His words were faint.

Anden pulled the dagger from his shoulder and the blade from his leg. Blood continued to seep out, but there was little he could do to treat it at the moment. "In better shape than you," he said.

Vargo squirmed in a pool of black liquid, having removed the object stuck in his neck. Anden recognized the item as the horn from the bolgia they fought at Kelveux. Vargo tried to crawl away until his strength waned and his body lay motionless. Taking his last breath, the assassin's foggy gaze lost no light as the life in them had left many years ago.

Anden retrieved his weapon. The corridor lurched forward, causing them both to collapse just short of Vargo's pool of blood. Anden assisted Damian to his feet, tossing an arm over his shoulder.

"What was that?" asked Damian.

"Wesley's working on grounding this thing," replied Anden. "He might be making some progress."

"There you are!" At the far end of the corridor was Wesley sprinting toward them. "Emperor be praised. You both look like you've been through hell," he said, approaching. He looked down at Vargo's dead body. "At least you managed to take that bastard out."

"A little help here," urged Anden.

Wesley hurried to Damian's other side, helping carry him through the hall. "We need to be making a swift departure," he said, quickening their pace. "This thing has got a one-way ticket for a very rough landing."

"And how do you propose we make our exit?" asked Damian.

"Same way we got up here."

They followed the corridor's outer wall until encountering a metal door similar to the one they entered. Cranking it open, the vicious wind tore into them as they crossed the grated walkway. Reaching the edge, Anden and Wesley each took hold of a rope while hooking their other arm around Damian's waist.

"On the count of three," yelled Anden, holding up three fingers for Wesley to see. "One... Two... Three!"

After the number left his lips, they leaped off the edge and descended toward the city. The fortress drifted past the mesa's edge, nosediving into the valley below. As the ground drew closer, the rope slipped from Anden's hand and brought all three of them crashing into the cobblestone. The sudden force squeezed the air out of his lungs and coated his body with numbness. Hardly able to move, Anden crawled toward Damian and Wesley, who lay still. Bleeding in the street, surrounded by ruins of buildings and ash, Anden considered this to be the end. No one would find them until the morning, and by then, he and Damian would most likely have bled out. By the looks of it, Wesley still had a chance, and that was good, considering he made an actual life for himself after they split up. As for Gwen, she had the keys to the chariot, and Wesley could still help her return home. It would be okay. He could die here, next to his friends. His brothers.

Through the lingering haze of smoke, a figure sprinted toward them. A woman wearing a tattered, orange sundress with a short sword strapped to her hip and dark, brown hair flowing through the air like a stream of chocolate. It was Gwen. Somehow, she had found them.

33

Run… Run… Run. The word echoed in Gwen's head. She didn't know where she was going and didn't care. The ruins of Danforth blurred past her as she raced through the streets. Her body propelled itself forward, acting of its own accord. She couldn't stop even if she wanted. A sizable piece of debris brought her to a halt as she tripped over it. Her legs skidded against the rocky surface of the cobblestone, tearing her sundress. She pulled herself to her feet and continued stumbling. Now stopped, her body found it difficult to force itself forward in a sprint. A metallic groan rumbled the sky as the nose of the hovering fortress tilted down. She kept searching, not wanting to rest until she found her allies. Heading in the same direction as the fortress through the fog of dust, she saw three shadows writhing on the ground. Getting closer, they took on the more solid form of Anden, Wesley, and Damian. She rushed to Anden's side, seeing him crawl.

"Wh— What… are you doing… here?" he asked. He was in rough shape, speaking between gasps for air. Damian and Wesley lay near him, barely moving.

"I came to find you," she said. "I don't know why, but I wanted to find you."

"I'm glad you did, I guess," he said, staggering up.

Gwen hurried to Wesley, who seemed to have received the least number of wounds. Shaking him, his eyes opened, and he sat up, clutching his side in pain.

"Gwen," he said in shock.

"It's alright." Tossing his arm around her, she pulled him to his feet. Once up, he limped over to Damian's body. The man was leaking blood from the same side of his previous wound. "What happened?" she asked.

"Got himself into a stupid fight," explained Anden. "We won, though, in the end."

An explosion erupted beyond the wall of the mesa. A large fireball flashed a bright light before fading into a pillar of smoke. The fortress no longer lingered over the city, now burning in a pile of metal. Damian's feet dragged against the ground as they carried him.

"You think we can make it through the sewers and back to the chariot?" Gwen grunted. She struggled to keep Damian's immense weight aloft.

Anden shook his head. "Not in our current state. Best to go back to the house and rest."

A man whose black hair faded into white at the fringes dug through the debris, opening a path to an alleyway. Seeing them, he approached to offer help but froze in fear as he lay eyes on Damian.

"T— T— The Burnt Coat," he stuttered, pointing a shaky finger. "That's the Burnt Coat."

"Help us, please," begged Gwen.

The man shook his head and spun around, taking off in the opposite direction. As he ran, she noticed the tattered image of a phoenix on the back of his jacket.

"We need to keep moving," said Anden.

They pressed on, eventually reaching the plaza. Water no longer flowed out of the fountain, and the statue standing over it lay on the ground, demolished. Hauling themselves into the house, they placed Damian on the floor. Gwen gathered as much cloth as she could and piled it onto his wound. She was no doctor, but she knew they needed to slow the bleeding. Wesley brought her rolls of thread and some needles he found lying around. Together, they clumsily stitched the wound closed and wiped it dry of any blood. It wasn't pretty, but it got the job done.

Wesley plopped into a chair and leaned on the kitchen table. He ate some of the meal he prepared. Gwen ate some too. It was cold and chewy but better than nothing. Anden sat on the floor, propped up against a wall. While they worked on Damian, he managed to patch himself up and cover the wound in his shoulder and leg.

"At least we did it," said Wesley.

Anden grabbed the bottle of liquor he'd brought in earlier. Uncorking it, he took a long swig. "Sure, but let's never do something like that again. From now on, my feet stay on solid ground."

"I can agree to that." Wesley took the bottle from Anden and chugged a few gulps before handing it back. "That shit did age well."

"Yeah, it did," said Anden with a longing look in his eye.

Gwen approached and snatched the bottle from Anden's grasp. Touching it to her lips, she downed three large gulps before pulling away. It burned her throat and chest, sending her into a fit of coughing. She leaned against the wall next to Anden. "You were right back at the capital when we first met. The world is shit."

He didn't respond.

"What are the chances that Noreen is dead?" she asked.

"I can't be entirely sure," he said, "but if she was in the guildhall, then pretty likely."

"So, what now? You plan on leaving me here come the morning?"

Anden stared at Damian's unconscious body sitting across from them. "We'll discuss that later. For now, we can rest."

He tilted his hat over his face. Wesley sprawled across the table, asleep. Gwen took one more drink from the bottle of liquor. Danforth was in ruin, and Noreen was most likely dead.

Her hopes of returning home were dashed away within a singular night. The only good thing was that the three men passed out around her were still alive. At this moment, she felt like they were the only ones she could trust. Whether or not they would still help her in the coming days had yet to be seen, but for tonight, they were here. With that comforting thought, Gwen, too, closed her eyes and released herself into a deep slumber. Perhaps, this was nothing more than a drawn-out dream. Upon waking, she may find herself back in her chambers at the palace overlooking the glorious white city of Alastair, but she doubted it.

Photo Credit: Nick Neumar

ABOUT THE AUTHOR

MITCHELL MOUNTAIN works as a full-time video editor
and enjoys storytelling of all kinds. Raised in Indiana, he
studied at Belmont University and graduated with a degree in
Motion Pictures.